A CAPFUL OF COURAGE

BOOK TWO OF THE NIGHTINGALE FAMILY SERIES

FENELLA J MILLER

B
Boldwood

First published in 2016 as *Count Your Blessings*. This edition first published in Great Britain in 2024 by Boldwood Books Ltd.

Cover Design by Colin Thomas

Cover Photography: Colin Thomas

The moral right of Fenella J. Miller to be identified as the author of this work has been asserted in accordance with the Copyright, Designs and Patents Act 1988.

A CIP catalogue record for this book is available from the British Library.

Paperback ISBN 978-1-83518-693-0

Large Print ISBN 978-1-83518-692-3

Hardback ISBN 978-1-83518-691-6

Ebook ISBN 978-1-83518-694-7

Kindle ISBN 978-1-83518-695-4

Audio CD ISBN 978-1-83518-686-2

MP3 CD ISBN 978-1-83518-687-9

Digital audio download ISBN 978-1-83518-689-3

Boldwood Books Ltd
23 Bowerdean Street
London SW6 3TN
www.boldwoodbooks.com

NOTE FROM THE AUTHOR

A Capful of Courage takes place between October 1843 and August 1844. An account of the opening of the Thames Tunnel is included in this story. Keen history buffs may know that this happened on 25 March 1843, but will hopefully forgive me for moving the date to provide a dramatic backdrop for Alfie's final adventures in London.

1

COLCHESTER, OCTOBER 1843

With the children tumbling around her and an infant to cradle, Sarah was right at home. Her bedroom had no fireplace but there was a thick rag rug across the boards, which kept out the draughts that came up through the gaps. There were faded curtains pulled across the window, and they helped to keep the room warm as well. What she wanted was her patchwork quilt and other bits and pieces from her friend Betty at Grey Friars House. Should she go round and collect them after she'd got the money from the bank? It would make the place seem more like home.

Home? She mustn't think like that. She couldn't stay in Colchester – she'd never get a decent job without references. She had almost ten pounds saved, but it wouldn't last forever if she wasn't working. She didn't want to dip into her nest egg too much – that was for her future. Some of it must be used to find herself decent lodgings whilst she looked for a suitable position. Much better to leave her belongings where they were, let Betty keep them whilst she got on with writing her own references.

She needed to plan her trip to London. If she took a coach she wouldn't have to walk three miles to the station, but the train only took a couple of hours, not all day to reach the city. Time enough to worry about that when she was ready to leave.

The house slowly quietened. The boys in the attic above her eventually stopped chattering. The church clock striking the hour kept her company during the long, sleepless night. When she left Colchester, as she must, she might never see Alfie again. He'd come back to look for her one day and she'd be gone. Once she was established in a decent position in London it might not be possible to return. She'd be lucky if she got a whole day off a quarter, and that was barely enough time to get to Colchester even on a train, let alone back again.

What was her brother doing at the moment? Was he happy? She prayed he'd had better luck than her, was prospering wherever he was. She rarely thought of her mother and stepfather now. They'd not considered her, so it was best she forgot them. She'd been around a few times to the churchyard and tidied up little Tommy's grave, put a few flowers in a pot under the simple wooden cross. She wished she could afford to get the stonemason to make him a headstone, but like other poor folk he'd have to make do with what was there.

Mrs Billings had told her she could eat breakfast with the family, or make her own with whatever was in the larder. The bank wouldn't let her withdraw her funds until the end of next week. That meant she had several extra days to spend in these unaccustomed surroundings. It wouldn't do to get settled. She must be off in a week or two.

She was determined to say goodbye to Betty before she left, but her friend didn't have an afternoon off until the end of November, which was nearly a month away. Should she stay until then? She had sufficient money in the bank to pay for her board and lodgings. Keeping herself busy helping out in the house would make time fly by. Mrs Billings didn't need the room back until January; it was just possible Alfie would reappear before she left.

Downstairs it was cold and dark, the range almost out, the house quiet, apart from the occasional wail from baby Beth Billings. She glanced at the clock in pride of place on the mantelshelf. It was not quite seven o'clock. Good grief! At Grey Friars House she'd have been at work an hour by now. Deciding to get things going, have breakfast ready and the table laid by the time Mrs Billings came down, Sarah set about finding what she needed.

She was used to being up at six, couldn't understand why people would want to waste the best part of the day lying in bed. Still, Mrs Billings didn't look too good. This pregnancy was clearly taking its toll on her. Well, after eight children, it was hardly surprising.

Her eyes filled. The mistress at Grey Friars would be having her sixth child in December, but she'd never see the baby, nor the children she'd taken care of for two years. Rich folk thought more about their servants being honest than the feelings of their children.

At last, the range was hot. It was time to put the kettle on and start making the porridge. She'd make some bread, and, if she could find the ingredients, do a batch of buns as well. The dough was proving on the back of the range, the porridge simmering on a hot plate, the table laid and the room swept before the clatter of small feet told her the boys were coming down for breakfast.

* * *

So the pattern of her days was established. Each morning it fell to her to get up first, do all the jobs Mrs Billings ought to be doing. It wasn't her place to do this, but she liked to be occupied and her landlady was so grateful she hadn't the heart to complain. Idleness didn't suit her; action took her mind away from the emptiness of her life. There was no point sending a note to Betty to ask her to meet up – her friend couldn't read, and there was no one else she could ask to pass on the message. It was too soon to ask the housekeeper for a favour.

No, that wasn't quite true – the gardener's boy had a soft spot for her. She was sure if she sneaked round the back and found him he'd get a message to Betty for her. She'd slip up there this afternoon, when Beth was taking her nap. Maybe the boys would like to come? They could run round the castle bailey if the gate was open.

'I'm going out to take a message to my friend, Ada. Is there anything you'd like me to get you whilst I'm out?'

'I could do with a few vegetables and perhaps some mutton for a stew. It's very good of you, Sarah, but it ain't right you doing all this, not when I should be doing it for you. I'll not charge you more than a shilling a week in future, just enough to pay for your food.'

'That would be a great help. I need to save as much as I can. I know I have to leave here when Mr Billings and your boys come back, but I want to have enough to take me to London when I do go.'

She wasn't planning to stay that long. Whatever had prompted her to say so?

'That'll be grand, Sarah love. The baby is due the beginning of January. I would be happier having someone else in the house around that time. The ship's not due until after that, so if you could stay with me, I would be ever so grateful.'

Sarah nodded. 'That's settled then. I'll pay you a shilling a week for my food, so you won't be out of pocket and I'll help out wherever I can. But I need some time for myself. I'm helping out, not working for you.'

'I know that, love – you're not my drudge. I hope you're my friend. I think of you like a daughter already. My twins must be the same age as you. They'd do the same if they was here.'

Taking the boys with her, wrapped up against the biting wind like woolly parcels, she set off for Queen Street, a large basket on her arm.

'I shall shop on the way back, Charlie. I don't want to lug things around with me until I have to.'

'I'll carry the basket when it's full, Sarah. Me ma says I must. I'm the man of the house whilst Pa and me big brothers are away.'

He reminded her of Alfie at that age. Her brother would be a man now – two years was a long time when you were still growing. Look at her, she'd turned from a girl to a woman. She noticed men turning to look as she walked past. That hadn't happened last year. And that Bert Sainty – their old neighbour in Colchester – he'd be eager to fumble under her clothes given half a chance.

After what happened to Jane, she'd steer clear of entanglements, keep her knees together like Betty had said. She smiled. Well, if a handsome young man, with his own house and a regular job should offer for her, she might reconsider. There was a lot to be said for the security of knowing where your next meal was coming from.

'Charlie, take your brothers and wait for me by the castle. The gates are locked today so you can't go in, but you can have a good look over the fence. I've got to take a message to the place where I used to work. Don't wander off – promise me now.'

'We won't, Sarah. We haven't been up here this year. Will there be time to walk down to the river before we go home?'

'I don't know. The wind's bitter, and look at those clouds. I think there might be snow coming; it's a bit soon for that, so I might be wrong. We don't want to get caught out in a snowstorm do we?'

Leaving the children arguing about the prospect of snow and whether a jaunt to the river was worth the risk of being caught in a blizzard, she hurried down the pathway. She kept the hood of her cloak down over her head in case anyone might recognise her. She slipped round the back, but instead of going to the door she went to the poultry house.

'Robbie, are you in here?'

The resulting clucks and squawks indicated he was there. 'Crikey! You don't want to be caught round here, Sarah. I can't be seen talking to you.'

'I'm not staying long. I need a small favour. Could you tell Betty to meet me her on her afternoon off? I'll wait by the castle. Will you do that for me, for old times' sake please? I'd be ever so grateful.'

He couldn't resist, not when she put on her widest smile. 'Just this once. I don't dare do it again – not even for you, Sarah Nightingale.'

She bent and kissed him lightly on his grubby cheek. That was reward enough, certainly the only payment *he* was going to get. With a whirl of skirts she hurried back to find the boys waiting obediently where she'd left them.

'Well, do we risk it? What you think, Charlie?'

'Not today, Sarah. Ma wouldn't like me brothers out in the snow. We still got the shopping to do ain't we?'

Sarah was relieved; the last thing she wanted was to trek down to the river. 'I think that's a wise decision, Charlie. You're a sensible boy. Now we have to buy provisions and there may be a copper spare to get you all a barley sugar twist as well.' This bribe was enough to make them forget the river.

Charlie insisted on carrying the basket. He was bent almost double by the weight, but didn't complain. She knew it would be wrong to take it from him; his pride would be hurt if she did.

They went down the side passage, through the gate in the wall and into the garden. She looked round – yes, it was definitely big enough to be considered a garden. There were flower beds down either side, a substantial vegetable patch and a few chickens in an enclosure at the far end next to the privy.

'Are there any eggs today, Charlie? I used the last making cakes this morning.'

'I'll go and have a look. They don't lay much now – I reckon it's the cold. And there ain't much to peck up off of the ground.' The boys ran down to the henhouse, leaving her to unlatch the kitchen door. Ada was rocking gently in a chair next to the range and there was no sign of the little one.

'We're back, Ada. The boys are looking for eggs. Is Beth having a nap?'

'She's just gone down. I'm having one meself. You go ahead, Sarah, don't worry about disturbing me. I'll doze in the chair. I reckon I'm that tired I could sleep through a thunderstorm.'

The boys burst into the kitchen, bringing a blast of icy air, and smoke puffed from the range. 'Close the door quickly. It's freezing out there. Was that snow in the air, Charlie?'

'It were, Sarah – it's coming down heavy now. We'll be able to build a snowman later.'

'I hate the stuff. It's cold, wet and creeps into your boots; but at least we've got enough in for the next few days. I'll not have to go marketing for a while.'

She wouldn't be able to go to the bank either, not if the weather was inclement. It wasn't worth risking a broken ankle and anyway she wasn't leaving Colchester until January now. The money was safe and she had nearly a pound in her bedroom, more than enough to tide her over.

* * *

Colchester, November 1843

Two weeks later the snow had thawed and the weather was back to the more usual grey and damp you'd expect for November. Sarah was concerned about Ada. She had no energy and her ankles were so swollen by the end of the day she could scarcely walk. Sarah suggested they got the midwife in, but Ada insisted she was fine and couldn't afford to pay out unnecessarily.

There had been a letter come from Mr Billings. Ada couldn't read but her husband was literate. Sarah read it to her. His ship was making good time and he expected to dock in Harwich in the middle of December, a month earlier than planned. He expressed a wish to be home when the baby arrived.

She was pleased, even though this meant she had to change her plans. A woman needed her man about the place when a baby was born. She would make arrangements to leave for London a bit sooner. When she went to meet Betty she'd go to the bank, withdraw her money and buy the necessary paper to forge her references. She'd not take the coach. Now the weather was bad she'd rather go on the train instead and not risk getting stuck in a ditch.

The grand houses in London could be looking for extra staff for the Christmas season. Hopefully she'd get something, even if it was temporary.

* * *

It was Friday, the day of the cattle and corn market in the high street. She'd have preferred to go on a quieter day, but this was Betty's free after-noon so there was no choice. At least she could be certain the bank would be open – on market days there would be a deal of money changing hands. She'd just have to be extra vigilant whilst carrying her life savings with her; there were bound to be ne'er-do-wells and pickpockets about as well.

Ada smiled sadly as Sarah was putting on her cloak. 'I'm going to miss you, Sarah love. I wish we had room, but there ain't. And anyway, Billings wouldn't like it if you were here. He's not too keen on strangers, my man ain't.'

'I'm going to miss you too, Ada, and the children. But we both knew I couldn't stay when your family returned. It's much better that you have your husband home when the baby comes. I'm glad I've been able to be of assistance. I'd better get off – my friend will be waiting. She only has three hours.'

She tied her bonnet securely, checked her hair was firmly pinned at the back of her neck, and pulled on her mittens. She'd sewn an extra pocket into her waistband. This had a drawstring top so she could drop her money in and pull it tight. There was no way a thief could dip in *there* and get it.

Several passers-by greeted her by name. She'd been living in the neighbourhood long enough to have become a familiar sight in the surrounding streets. She had visited Mrs Cooke the first week to thank her for giving her Ada's address. She'd been round a couple of times since to take her a batch of cakes.

Sarah had been shocked to find the old lady lived in a neglected cottage, the limewash on the walls all but gone, the fire barely adequate to keep out the cold. No wonder Annie trudged up to the Wednesday fruit and vegetable market to buy the leftovers. She'd visit again before she left the area and put a couple of pennies in with the cakes next time.

She'd not dwell on that; she had to think of herself, look to the future. She was determined to be optimistic, believe she would find herself suitable employment without spending all her savings. She would come back next spring to collect her belongings, see Betty, check if her brother had returned, and nip down to visit with Ada and the boys and see the new baby.

Although a day wasn't long, on the train it could be done. Mind, she'd have to find employment on the east side of the city; crossing London might well take longer than the fifty miles to Colchester.

She reached the corner of Queen Street and was shocked to find East Hill full of livestock, the bellowing and lowing of the cattle all but deafening. The street was littered with fresh dung and she was obliged to wait a good fifteen minutes whilst the drover herded the two dozen cattle down the hill. Betty was waiting for her, her face wreathed in smiles.

'I was beginning to think you wasn't never getting across, Sarah. You look well. I've been that worried about you since you went, but I can see you've found yourself somewhere decent to live.'

'I have, with a Mrs Billings. She lives just off St Botolph's Street. I've been helping her out, cooking and cleaning and so on. I've only to pay a shilling a week. But her husband and boys are coming home soon, so I've got to move on. That's why I wanted to see you, to say goodbye.'

Betty flung her arms around her. 'Sarah, don't leave Colchester. Even if we can't meet often at least I'll know you're there.'

'I have to. I'm going to write myself some references, and I'm not stupid enough to try and use them anywhere that the master's name would be recognised.'

'Then it has to be London? Ain't Chelmsford far enough?'

'No, I have to go somewhere no one has ever heard of Mr Bawtree. I'm going to draw my money from the bank today and buy the paper and envelopes to do the references. Tell me, what's been happening at Grey Friars in my absence?'

'You'll never guess – Sally's been sacked. She was caught pinching by Nanny Brown not long after you left. There's a new under nurse now, but she's not a patch on you, I can tell you. Still, that's not your concern. Let's get going. Shall we go to The Red Lion? If you're getting your money from the bank, you can treat me to a pot of tea and a cake.'

Sarah laughed at Betty's cheek. 'I'll do that, but I want to ask you a favour. Can you keep my things until I come down for them next year? Now there's the train, I've worked out I could get there and back in a day. I'll write and then you can get Mrs Hall to read it; I think she might be prepared to pass on a message by then.'

'I reckon she would. I heard her talking to Cook the other day, saying it was a shame you had to go, as you were the best girl she'd employed in years.' Betty grinned and squeezed her arm. 'I ain't told you the best bit – I've been keeping it for last.'

'Go on then, you're fair bursting to tell me.'

'I'm the under nurse. That's why I said she wasn't a patch on you. Nanny asked if I could have the job, and Madam agreed. I'm on a month's trial. I reckon I've done all right and I'll hear next week if my position's permanent.'

Sarah wasn't sure if she was pleased or envious of her friend's success. 'I'm glad for you, Betty. You deserve promotion and I'm sure you'll get good news. Did you move into my old room?'

'I certainly did. I've got your things hidden in the back of the chest. The two nursery-maids don't dare come in. They're willing enough, but neither of them are much more than children themselves.'

'How are the children? No, tell me when we're having our tea. I must go to the bank. I won't be able to afford to treat you if I haven't got my money. I didn't bring anything with me.'

Sarah joined the queue at the counter, her bank book ready for when it was her turn. The clerk handed out the money without a murmur; she was the proud possessor of nine pounds eight shillings. It was a small fortune, more than enough to keep her out of the workhouse for a year or two even if she couldn't find employment. She was tempted to put some back, collect it when she returned, but there was a press of people behind her and she didn't want to draw attention to herself.

Surreptitiously she slipped the money into its special hiding place. With her cloak wrapped tightly around her, she was certain no one would notice the small bulge. She kept out a pound to pay for her train ticket and writing materials. She also wished to purchase small Christmas gifts for the Billings family, and something for the new baby as well.

Inside The Red Lion a huge log fire burnt brightly in the snug, but it was surrounded by farmers and traders. There was no room for them to find a table and order themselves a hot drink. The comments from the men made her cheeks turn red. In her haste to escape she trod on Betty's toes.

'We should have realised, it's too busy for us in here. Where can we go? We need to think of somewhere the farmers won't be, somewhere a bit further away from the market.'

'What about Mr Doe's Temperance Hotel in Wire Street at the back of The Red Lion? We can go through the yard here, then cut down Lion Walk easy enough.'

Sarah wasn't too happy about taking this route, not when she was carrying so much money. She'd be happier staying on the main thoroughfare where there were people around, someone you could call out to if you were set upon.

'Look, Sarah, over there. I think that's Sally. She's got two blokes with her – surely she's not on the game already?'

'Quickly, I don't like the look of those men. Betty, they've seen us. They're coming over.' Sarah wished they hadn't come this way. It was far too quiet.

2

Sarah gathered up her skirts and ran, praying that Betty had the sense to follow. The sound of running feet behind her was reassuring, then she realised it wasn't Betty. She increased her pace. They were closer, too close. A blow from behind sent her stumbling forward to crash painfully on her knees. Instinctively she curled into a tight ball, protecting her precious money within the cradle of her body.

'No point in trying keep it, you stuck-up bitch,' a rough voice hissed in her ear. 'You've been to the bank. We've been watching out for you these past weeks. Give it us or we'll take it as hard as you like.'

They were not going to steal her money without a fight. Where was Betty? There'd been no cry. Had they struck her to the ground as well?

Her knees were bleeding, but so far she'd suffered no serious injury. Should she meekly hand over her money to avoid being hurt? Never! She had on heavy boots, when they came near she would lash out. If she screamed maybe someone would come to her assistance. She tugged off her mittens, needing her hands free to scratch and gouge where she could.

Rough hands gripped her shoulders and shook her like a rat in a terrier's mouth. Her head jerked painfully from side to side and finally cracked against the wall. Dizzy from this treatment, but still conscious, she lashed out wildly, her feet making contact several times. It was a bad decision. Her actions enraged her attackers and a series of punches rained down on her. She screamed, but no one came. Then a final blow sent her spinning into blackness.

From somewhere far away a voice was calling her name. 'Sarah, Sarah, have they killed you? I've called the constables – someone's coming to help you. Be still until they arrives.'

It was her friend. Slowly she forced open her bruised eyes. Every bit of her hurt, and her mouth was full of blood, several of her teeth could be loosened. The waistband of her skirt was ripped apart, the money gone; even the pound she'd had in her cloak pocket had been stolen. Despair overwhelmed her. She closed her eyes again, willing the blackness to take her back.

They'd taken everything she owned. She was destitute, only a few shillings between her and the workhouse.

Betty called her repeatedly, but Sarah made no effort to respond. She wished she could die; she had no hope left. Unfamiliar voices were arguing above. A man spoke firmly to someone she couldn't hear.

'I ain't leaving this poor girl to freeze to death on the pavement. You two take the money back to Mr Hawkins. I'm stopping here to help.'

Sarah tried to sit up. She didn't want this man to lose his employment because he'd been kind enough to come to her assistance. 'I'll be all right in a minute; my friend can help me when I've got my breath back.'

A warm coat, smelling of wood shavings and tobacco, dropped around her shoulders. 'I'm Dan Cooper. Can you put your arm around my neck? I'll soon have you somewhere warm and dry.'

Strong arms lifted her from the freezing cobbles. Betty tucked the jacket tight. She wanted to protest but her head flopped onto the man's shoulder. She had no energy left and welcomed the darkness as it took her once more.

The overpowering smell of carbolic and the rattle of pans finally dragged her to consciousness. She must be in a bed in the hospital in Lexden Road. Ma had always said only a handful of those who went into hospital ever came out alive. Suddenly she didn't want to be one of the many, but one of the few who survived. She opened her eyes and pushed herself onto her elbows; a wave of agonising pain washed over her. She bit back her moan.

Betty was at her bedside, face chalk white and tear-streaked. 'Sarah, thank the good Lord. I thought you dead a while back.'

Sarah forced her broken mouth to smile. 'I'm battered and bruised, but I'll live. Where have they taken my clothes? I need them back. I'm not stopping here – I'm going back to Ada's. I'll stay there until I get well and can find myself some sort of work.'

Betty nodded. 'The constables were here. I told them what happened. That bitch Sally and her brothers took your money. She tripped me up, and sat on me so I couldn't get up and help you; but I saw it all and the police know where to look. I reckon they'll catch them and you'll get your money back.'

'I won't. They might catch the thieves, but the money will be gone. I'm destitute. I can't go to London. I'll have to find myself somewhere else to live before Mr Billings comes back and throws me out.'

'Don't worry about that now. You're not in any fit state to go back to your lodgings. Don't cost you nothing to be in hospital. It's charity, right? You stop and get fed here. You can't expect the landlady to take care of you, not like you are.'

It was almost dark; Betty should be back at Grey Friars. If she was tardy on her first afternoon off since her promotion, she might not get her position confirmed after her month's trial. 'Betty, you're a good friend, but you must go. Take care of my things. I'll send word before long. Go, before you're late.'

'All right; that Dan Cooper took a real shine to you. He carried you all the way here, and he's coming tomorrow to see how you are. He said he'd do for those two what did it. I reckon if the law don't find Sally and her brothers he and his mates will.'

'I don't remember much about it, but he put his jacket round me, didn't he?'

'He did that, quite enjoyed the sight of him in his shirtsleeves. Lovely broad shoulders and a fine head of curly black hair. Getting on a bit, about four and twenty I reckon. If I was you, my girl, I'd hang on here until he comes back. He might be the answer to your prayers.'

In spite of her desolation and injuries Sarah smiled. Trust Betty to think of something like that. 'I'm sixteen; far too soon to be thinking about that sort of thing. Anyway, if he's as old as you say, he'll be married already with a family to provide for.'

Reluctantly her friend gathered up her possessions, leaning over to give her a kiss. She promised to come down and visit as soon as she had time off. 'I know you won't be with Mrs Billings, but she'll know where you are.' The handsome stranger was not mentioned again.

Sarah didn't disagree. By the time the seasonal festivities were over she'd be long gone. She had no intention of telling Ada where she planned to live; she didn't want anyone coming round to the slums where she was heading.

A nurse brought her a bowl of tasty broth and a cup of tea. She mumbled her way through both, and explained why she would like her clothes. Her tale was nothing new, and with her gone there'd be an empty bed for the next casualty.

The woman understood. Her clothes were fetched, but she needed assistance to an get them on. They were muddy, still wet from the time she'd spent spreadeagled on the cobbles. Fortunately, apart from the wrecked waistband of her skirt they were undamaged. The nurse told her she was lucky not to have been raped. Sarah didn't feel the slightest bit lucky.

Somehow she staggered back down St John's Road. She was exhausted when she reached her destination. Using the walls of the narrow passageway to hold herself upright, she unlatched the gate and tottered to the back door. Charlie opened it; his face fell. 'Ma, Sarah's come back. She's been beaten up something bad.'

Ada insisted she took the rocking chair by the fire, fussing and worrying about the awful ordeal Sarah had suffered. 'It could have been worse – you know what I mean. What you've lost can be replaced. Thank the good Lord for that.'

'So I've been told. I was too busy fighting for my money to worry about my virtue. I'd no idea *that* sort of thing happened in Colchester.'

'It happens everywhere, Sarah love. You're welcome to stay here right up until my Frank comes home. I don't expect you to help until you're better. Here, Charlie, you get Sarah up to her room. He'll bring you what you want on a tray tomorrow. I'll not have you put out on the streets just before Christmas; I'll make sure I find you somewhere.'

It took three days for Sarah to feel well enough to resume what she considered as her duties. She'd got precisely nineteen shillings and sixpence, more than a lot of folk had where she was intending to go. It wasn't much, but she'd make it last. She'd find herself a cheap room somewhere in St Botolph's Parish. It was the poorest part of town, jammed with little lanes, alleys and courtyards. It would be vile, but unless she was prepared to pawn Alfie's watch, she had no option.

When Ada came down to find the bread baking, the porridge bubbling and the tea made, she smiled gratefully. 'You're stronger than I thought, Sarah love. I reckon you'll survive wherever you are. Most women would have gone under after the beating you took, and losing your life savings, but not you.' She collapsed into her rocking chair. The boys settled themselves around the table and Sarah took Beth on her lap to feed her.

'I've sent Charlie to see old Annie; she's going to ask around for you. You must visit her today, see what she's found out.'

Charlie noisily scraped up the last of his porridge. Ada waited for her reaction.

'That's kind of you and Charlie. I don't think I'll venture out until this afternoon. I'm still a little unsteady but I'm sure I shall be better later.'

However, the weather worsened, not snow but icy rods of rain. Snow would be preferable – at least it didn't drench a body to the bone the moment they stepped outside. She had no choice. She could be turned out of her comfortable room any day; she had to have somewhere to go when that happened.

'If it's all right with you, Ada, I'm going along to see Annie. I'd hoped the rain would ease off, but I daren't wait any longer.'

'You'll get drenched, but that can't be helped I suppose. When you get back you can dry your clothes in front of the fire. You don't want to leave with wet things.'

Sarah put on the garments she'd worn when she'd been attacked. She'd brushed them, but they were still dirty and she'd not had the energy to launder them. She might as well get them wet, and wash them properly tomorrow.

It was not far to Annie's home, but even in the fifteen minutes it took her she was soaked through. 'Here you are then, lovie. Sorry to hear about your attack, but the bruises will fade soon enough.' She stepped back and Sarah ducked her head and followed her into the cottage.

'Charlie Billings said you might have heard of somewhere suitable. I'd like to be able to see it before I take it, try and get it clean before I move in. I might only have a few more days where I am.'

'I'd ask you to lodge here, but I've already got me two regulars staying. I sleep by the fire when they're with me. I ain't sure you can go round until you take the room. It ain't like staying with Ada Billings you know.'

Thankfully the fire was more substantial than usual, in honour of the lodgers no doubt. 'Is it all right to hang my cloak by the fire?' The old lady nodded and poured Sarah a cup of tea.

'This'll warm you up. Put yourself on the stool. You look right poorly; the last thing you want is to get congestion of the lungs.'

'I'm sorry I haven't brought you any cakes today. Ada's not charging me anything for my board so I can't expect her to pay for extras.'

'Don't you fret, my girl – you've done more than enough for me already. It's me what owes you a favour, and I ain't let you down. I've been asking around, and there's a couple of places vacant. Mind you, that was two days ago. They could have been taken by now.'

'Where are they?'

'I ain't sure exactly. You've to go to The Prince of Wales, ask to speak to Ma Peck. She's the landlady there, but she's agent for Mr Hatch – collects the rents and that. She'll find you something suitable; she's a good sort. Mind you, it won't be what you're used to, but beggars can't be choosers.'

'I shall be grateful to have any sort of roof over my head. I only have a few shillings left, and I don't suppose any of those rooms will have furniture in.'

The old lady cackled. 'Bless you, course they don't. You'll need something to sleep on, a couple of blankets and a chair. I asked particular about rooms with a fireplace – you'll want to be able to do a bit of cooking.'

'I won't have enough to buy all that, not until I find myself some work. I don't care what I do as long as it brings me in a shilling or two. I don't suppose you've heard of anything going?'

'I ain't; sorry, love. But Ma Peck might know of something. Ask her when you go up there.'

'Well, it won't be today. I shall wait until I'm feeling better, unless I'm forced out earlier.'

Sarah said her farewells, promising to call in when she was settled. Annie might be the only friend she had once she'd left the security of Ada's house. Her cloak was still sodden, but then so were her clothes. The rain had eased off a little. She would hurry, try and keep warm that way.

Feeling a little more hopeful about the future she stepped into the kitchen to be faced by a giant of a man. He didn't look best pleased to see her. The house was silent, no sign of Ada or the children. She supported herself against the door, her heart pounding painfully. Mr Billings had come back too soon; she wasn't ready to go. Her clothes were wet and dirty, and she had no room arranged.

'You're not welcome here. Get upstairs and get your things out of my boys' room. My wife had no right to take you in without my say-so.'

There was no point protesting. This bad-tempered sailor had made up his mind. Without a word she stepped round him, her chin up, determined not to show her fear. Where *was* everyone? Surely he hadn't sent them out in this weather? And what about the two older boys? Had they been on the same ship as their father?

She expected her room to be ransacked but it was as she'd left it an hour ago. There wasn't much to do – her carpetbag was already half full. The remaining money was already stitched into the lining of her cloak. Even the most determined footpad would never find it there. As she dropped her toiletries on top of her clothes something chinked. Pushing aside the items she'd packed earlier she saw a small cloth purse. Ada had given her a few coins extra, something she could ill afford.

Her eyes filled. There were wicked people in the world. Life was mostly unfair for poor folk like her, but there were also kind and loving folk who were prepared to give their last penny to help someone worse off than themselves. Betty, Annie, Ada and Dan Cooper – they'd all been prepared to help her.

When Frank Billings returned to sea next year she would return, thank Ada, see if there was anything she could do in return. However, that was a long time in the future. For the moment she had to concentrate on her own survival, find herself a room, get employment, and one way or the other remain alive until the spring.

On impulse Sarah decided to leave by the front door. She wouldn't give that man the satisfaction of seeing her evicted. Clutching her carpetbag to her chest she pulled her wet cloak around it. She might look as if she was expecting. Even the most hardened criminal would think twice about attacking a girl in the family way.

It took some time to locate The Prince of Wales. It was mid-afternoon, but almost dark already. The streets were quiet even here. The smell coming from one side of the building made her gag; men must relieve themselves somewhere round there.

She pushed open the door and was surprised to see clean sawdust on the floor, the few tables and chairs polished and the serving hatch as clean as a new pin. This wasn't like The Bugle Horn, although most of the customers were just as noxious. There were a few men supping their drinks, but no women. Her cheeks coloured – she should have gone around the back. Women didn't enter beerhouses, not respectable ones anyway. Curious eyes bored into her back, and she stiffened her spine as she walked across to the hatch.

She heard a noise behind the heavy bead curtain and a tall, thin woman, hair scraped back in a knot on top of her head, came through. Her high-necked brown dress had long sleeves and made her look more like a housekeeper than an innkeeper.

'I'm Sarah. Annie Cooke said I was to call and enquire about a room.'

The woman gestured for her to come through the curtain, lifting it aside for her, and Sarah walked through, glad to be out of the bar. The woman's living quarters were spotless. If this woman could keep herself and her premises as clean as this when surrounded by filthy hovels and even filthier customers, she must do the same.

'There's two still free. One has a fireplace – it's dearer, mind, but you'd be better there if you can afford it.'

'I'll take it. I have a bit of money left, and I'm hoping to find work. I don't suppose you need anyone here?'

The woman looked her up and down and then smiled. 'It ain't pleasant work. I keeps the place clean enough but I ain't got no control over them that drink in here. One of me girls is off sick. You can take her place until she's back. It'll be busy over the festive season – folks like to drown their sorrows.'

Sarah couldn't believe she'd been able to find herself somewhere to live and paid employment within minutes of being thrown out. She must have a guardian angel after all. 'I'll take it. I've not done this sort of work, but I was in service before I lost my position. I'm a hard worker, and don't care what I do...' No, that was untrue. There was one thing she'd never contemplate, even if she was starving. 'I'm... I mean I don't...'

Ma Peck nodded. 'I didn't think you did. I'd not of taken you on if I thought you'd spread your legs for any Tom, Dick or Harry. This is a respectable establishment. None of my girls are on the game.' She smiled grimly. 'Mind you, the one what's sick is in the family way and no sign of the father anywhere.'

Sarah's optimism faded. She was out of her depth, had no idea how to manage in a place like this. The men who drank here were like those who had stolen her money. Although she might be safe when she was working, what about when she had to walk home in the dark through the stinking alleys to wherever her pitiful new lodgings might be? Who would look out for her then?

3

Ma Peck flung open the back door and shouted into the yard. 'John, I've got a young lady in here that's taking the room in the walk behind Bakers Row, off Magdalen Street. She needs someone to take her there. She'll never find it on her own and I'm short-staffed here.'

John Peck was a burly man, a fringe of gingery-brown hair around a bald pate. His eyes were kind, his cheeks rosy as polished apples. Sarah liked him on sight.

'Thank you, sir. I'm sorry to be a trouble, especially when the weather's so bad.'

'I never mind a bit of rain. I'll be happy to show you.' He shook his head, his lips pursed, and he stared sideways at his wife. 'Don't you have anything better? She's a sight too refined for the likes of them round there.'

Sarah quickly intervened. 'I shall manage, Mr Peck; I have so little money at the moment I must be satisfied with what's available. When I'm working, I can put a little by and find something better in the spring.'

'You got a job around here?'

Sarah looked for confirmation but Mrs Peck shook her head slightly. 'I've heard of something but I've to look into it yet. I'd like to get to my room, if that's not putting you out. I expect there's nothing in it, and I'll have to be out again and buy the necessities before it's too late.' It would be very unwise to be abroad in that neighbourhood at night.

Mr Peck insisted on carrying her carpetbag. He shrugged on a voluminous cloak and rammed on his felt hat.

Mrs Peck beckoned to her as they were leaving. 'You can start tomorrow. Be here at eight sharp. I'll give you the first shift. It's rough enough around here in the daytime and I'll not have my John complaining about you having to walk home at night. Taken a real shine to you, he has.'

Sarah smiled her thanks and hurried after him; first Mr Cooper, now Mr Peck. She must appeal to the older man. She needed a man's protection for her first foray into the slums that existed around Magdalen Street. The area was rife with prostitutes, lowlifes and thieves. She hoped there were others like her, women fallen on hard times, and that she wouldn't be totally surrounded by miscreants.

Since the barracks had been torn down after Waterloo the soldiers had gone – she wasn't sure if that was of benefit to her or not. Would military men have been more or less likely to accost her in the street? When full of beer no doubt they were just like any other man, foul-mouthed and vulgar; also a soldier would be trained to kill, would not think twice about taking what he wanted. The warning from both Ada, and the nurse at the hospital, about the possibility of being raped was constantly in her mind.

With the hood of her cloak pulled tightly over her head it served two purposes: it kept her precious bonnet secure and hid her face from curious passers-by. Even in her muddied garments she was a deal better dressed than the majority she met. In spite of the appalling conditions, children huddled on street corners and cowered in archways, their clothes little better than rags. Huge eyes stared hopelessly out of gaunt, white faces; the thought of such little ones living in hardship without shoes or warm clothing filled her with anguish.

It wasn't right that people like those she'd once worked for lived in such luxury, threw away more each day than people round here had in a month. Someone ought to do something about it. Wasn't that what Parliament was for? Shouldn't someone be speaking up for the downtrodden and doing something to improve their lot?

Her lips twitched. She was becoming a radical. She'd read pamphlets written by the Chartists but had never thought she would experience what they were protesting about. The downturn in her fortunes made her aware of how things were for those unable to earn enough to live on. Looking back, her life in East Stockwell Street had been one of comparative luxury and comfort.

Magdalen Street was busy. Small roadside stalls sold tired vegetables, the pieman could be heard shouting his wares further down the street. There was a baker's shop, a general store and what could pass for a haberdasher's. These were not like the shops she was used to; they were little more than oddments set out in the window of a cottage. No doubt folks around here made a penny where they could.

There seemed to be as many beerhouses as food stores. It was small wonder the children were so thin if their parents spent what little money they had on gin and beer. Victuals would be purchased by those returning from work. With luck the shops would remain open until late, at least until she had found what she needed.

Many in this neighbourhood would be dayworkers, would spend what they had on the way home. Judging from the noise coming from the bars they passed, most of it went down the men's throats. Were the women obliged to wait to intercept their husbands in order to get any housekeeping?

'The walk we want is down here, miss. Mind where you step. Folk aren't too fussy what they throw out in these parts.'

Her stomach lurched. She clamped her teeth shut and swallowed vigorously. She must endeavour to get used to the stench. There was no point in pretending she was still the old Sarah Nightingale. Now she was another destitute young woman hoping to stay alive by any means she could. They turned right and left and then into an even more noisome alley, the houses so close together they seemed to be at loggerheads. A large man could touch both sides of the street with his arms outstretched.

Her guide stopped at a building at the end of the row with slightly less filth piled up outside than the others. The doorstep was clean, as were the windows, and the curtains, although faded, had been washed recently.

'Your room is in here. You've only got people on the left of you, so it's quieter than most.'

Sarah prayed her room might be the one with the clean glass and the curtains. Even looking out onto another house would be better than no window at all.

He put his shoulder to the door. It didn't need a lock; you'd have to be a strong man to open it. God knows how she would manage on her own. Why did no one see to it? The door had swollen with the rain. Surely it wouldn't be too difficult to rehang it so it closed properly? What nonsense! This was a different world, where doors didn't fit and nobody cared enough to mend them.

The passageway caused Mr Peck to turn sideways. 'You're lucky, miss, your room's at the back, got a bit more privacy than the ones in front. You want to keep it locked at night mind. Although the lodgers in here are a bit cleaner than next door, they ain't nothing special, I can tell you.'

They shuffled past the stairwell. Sarah shuddered, relieved she didn't have to negotiate the narrow, twisting staircase. The smells that wafted down were almost as bad as the street. Human waste and unwashed bodies predominated. She'd just have to get used to it.

The key seemed overlarge for such a humble dwelling. It would be a nuisance carrying this about with her all the time. Mr Peck turned it easily. Thank God her room would be secure at night, her few belongings safe during the day whilst she was working.

'Right then, miss, it's not much, but better than nothing.'

He was obliged to step into the room so that she could see what was to be her home for the foreseeable future. Nothing had prepared her; her worst imaginings could not have conjured up such a dismal place. The window, if you could call it such, was no more than a foot square and so high on the wall it would be impossible to look out. Anyway it was thick with dirt. It might as well be midnight outside, the amount of light that came in through it.

Her companion had reached into his jacket pocket and removed a candle stub. Expertly flicking one of the matches against the wall, he lit it. By this single flickering light she surveyed the reality. The room was little more than the size of a store cupboard at Grey Friars; it *did* have a fire-place, but it was scarcely big enough for cooking. It might be possible to boil a small saucepan of water to make tea, and toast crumpets in front of the flames, but she'd never be able to make herself a meal.

The floor had no boards. It was beaten earth, the damp and cold already seeping up through the soles of her boots. There was no furniture; the previous tenant had left nothing, not even a hook on the wall to hang her cloak on. She'd be better off in the workhouse than living here. Unable to speak, she held out her hand for her bag.

'I know it's not what you're used to, but look at it this way: it's so small even that piddling fire will keep you warm. You won't need much furniture, a couple of rugs across the floor, a bed and some nails to hang your clothes and you'll be all set.' On this cheery note he turned to go.

Panic engulfed her. She didn't want to be left in this dreadful place, had no idea how to proceed, where to go to buy herself what she needed. Did she even have enough money? She couldn't begin to find the way back to the main thoroughfare. She'd rather throw herself on the parish than remain here.

'Mr Peck, please don't leave me. I can't live here; I won't be able to manage. I'll go along to Balkerne Lane. At least they'll give me a bed and regular food in there.'

He reached out and squeezed her shoulder. 'You don't want go in there, not really. It's the shock talking; I know your sort. Girls like you can manage if they set their minds to it. I knew you were a survivor the minute I set eyes on you. Now tell me what you want, and I'll go and buy it.'

'That's kind of you, but I can't stay here. There's nothing I can do until I've got some furniture. I haven't thought this through. I haven't even a bucket for collecting water.'

'You want three really: one for water, one for coal and one for you know what. You don't want to use the privy in the yard, not if you can help it.'

'What about the water? Where do I get that?'

'That's one thing in Colchester – at least we got pure water. You'll not catch anything from drinking the water from your pump. It's out back. It's another thing you share with this row of houses.' He stuffed her carpetbag into the empty grate so it wouldn't get damp on the floor. 'The water's on all day. You can go out when you want.'

She leant against the wall, the damp plaster making a cold patch between her shoulders. She had to be strong. After all, she had a few shillings in her pocket and was to start work the next day. She was a lot better off than some. If she kept her health, she would get through this and reach better times ahead.

'I'm steady now, sir. I have ten shillings to spend on furniture and food. I've paid a month in advance for this room and I'm keeping three shillings back. Will that be enough to get what I need?'

'More than enough. There's a second-hand yard in Magdalen Street that will have most of what you want. Here, take your key; you must lock the door. It's up to you to take care of yourself from now on.'

As they retraced their steps she took more notice of the landmarks. The walks appeared to be nameless; no doubt the post was never delivered in this area, so a real address wasn't needed. The wind had dropped, which was a blessing. She had an hour or so to get herself sorted out before the shops closed. Whatever she did to it, the room would never be her home.

* * *

Sarah frowned as she reviewed the improvements she had made. The room was less depressing certainly, but would always be little more than a furnished broom cupboard. However, she believed she had made a friend in Mr Peck. He was a true gentleman. He might be rough-speaking, but he had a heart of gold. His good offices had meant she'd been able to acquire so much for so little.

She'd bought a china basin and jug, a rickety deal table and bentwood chair, a chamber pot and various pieces of cutlery and crockery. Mr Peck had cajoled the furniture seller into lending him a handcart. On this he'd wheeled back a bed frame, a new straw-filled mattress, two blankets and two dented buckets. He'd promised to come round first thing the following day with wood and a handful of nails to construct a shelf for her.

She had to be at work by eight. She'd be obliged to leave before he got there and this would mean handing over the key when they met in the street. On their second jaunt he purchased her a sack of coal. He'd insisted on paying for it, telling her it was much cheaper to buy it in bulk than by the bucketful. This was propped against the wall, alongside was kindling and half a dozen tallow candles. By standing precariously on her chair she managed to clean the tiny window. It wouldn't make much difference but things ought to be clean.

The square of tatty carpet, cadged for a few pennies by her benefactor, was against the damp earth, the two rag rugs on top; with her boots on it was like walking on a normal floor. The rudimentary bed frame would not support a heavier person; she would have to remember not to toss about at night. Her blankets were clean but threadbare. She'd have to place her cloak across as well if she was to stay warm. She couldn't afford to have the fire alight all the time.

With her first wages she'd purchase a length of material and make herself a bag. If she kept her spare underwear inside it would do very well as a pillow. Even the small saucepan took an age to boil. Her cracked china mug held a spoonful from a twist of tea. It was more dust than leaves, but better than nothing. Her stomach gurgled in anticipation of the hot meat pie she'd treated herself to for supper. Tomorrow she'd be on short commons; she wasn't going to dip into her last three shillings in order to buy herself food. From now on she'd rely on the meal that was included in her wages at The Prince of Wales.

Mr Peck was right – there was something to be said for having this room. She *was* warm. The flickering light of the candle, plus the flames from the fire, were enough to dry her sodden garments.

She'd draped the wet clothes over the edge of the table and across the back of the chair. They'd not be laundered now. How did people manage to keep themselves fresh in these hovels? Laundering anything but the smallest items would be impossible. That was the least of her worries; she was fortunate to have a clean gown folded neatly on the table and the

requisite underwear. She was better off than many, and she thanked God
for it.

* * *

The clock at St Leonard's Church on Hythe Hill struck six. It was still
dark, too early to get up. She couldn't afford to light the fire and it was
much warmer in bed. A little after seven she washed in cold water, put her
hair up by touch alone. This was the first time she'd attempted this
without a glass to help her. With gritted teeth she removed her chamber
pot from under the bed. It wasn't the emptying that bothered her; it was
where it had to be emptied.

She had not stepped out of her room since her return the night before.
One or two residents had already been outside to relieve themselves but
no one was in the yard at the moment. The house was noisy: doors slamming, children crying and the shuffling and banging of feet on bare
boards. During the night there'd been a disturbance next door; a hideous
domestic argument, a woman screaming, the sounds of blows and a man's
voice raised in anger. The walls were thin. Nobody could have any secrets
living here.

That poor woman – to be woken by a drunken husband and beaten
for no apparent reason. The married state was not for her. She didn't have
the worry of children, or the fear of being mistreated. All she had to do
was take care of herself and that suited her just fine.

Alfie would come back next year; together they'd make themselves a
decent life. She would keep house; he'd bring her in a wage to supple-
ment whatever she could earn. This was a daydream, she knew, but Mrs
Hall had been fond of saying that it was good to have something to
aim for.

A year ago her goal had been to save enough from her wages to set
herself up in her own business, or take charge of a nursery in a grand
house in the country. How things had changed. Now, it was to stay alive
until her brother returned to Colchester.

So far she'd avoided a visit to the privy but she could have found her
way blindfolded. The smell, even in the cold, was enough to kill a horse

stone dead. It was impossible to hold her nose and carry the pot, so she held her breath instead. This meant the hem of her skirts trailing in the mud; it was small wonder everyone looked dishevelled.

She opened the door. The hole in the seat was so repellent she almost tipped the contents on her boots. Stepping forward she emptied her doings, glad she'd not had any breakfast. The scuttling of rats made the experience even more unpleasant, if that were possible. The night soil men should be called; this privy hadn't been emptied for a month. There was no way on God's earth she'd ever sit over one of those stinking holes. Heaven knows what might come up!

After slamming the door, she gathered her skirts and hurried to the communal pump further down the yard. Rinsing her empty receptacle under the freezing water, she was just glad she'd completed this unpleasant task before anyone had observed her embarrassment. The pot vanished under the bed. She washed her hands and dried them on the cloth that served as a towel. There, that was the worst of the jobs done. She was just exiting when, to her surprise, Mr Peck turned up.

'Good morning, sir, so kind of you to help me out in this way.'

He beamed, his jowls wobbling. 'Ma tells me you're to work in the bar. It ain't the sort of work a girl like you should be doing, but needs must, I suppose. She'll keep an eye on you, and if anyone misbehaves, I'll flatten them.'

'I have to leave, Mr Peck, or I shall be late. That wouldn't do on my first day.'

'I've had a word with the missus. You're to come back with me today. Just you sit down out the way, and I'll get on. I'll have a fine shelf, with hooks underneath to hang mugs and such, and a few nails in the wall for your clothes, in no time.'

She felt a glow of happiness. Her situation was dire, but this man's kindness gave her hope. After a deal of hammering and banging the work was done. 'That's a splendid job – I have everything I need.'

He chuckled and pushed his tools into his bag. 'We'd best be off now, miss. Won't do to keep Ma waiting any longer.' He gestured to her clean dress. 'She'll be pleased you've made an effort. Raise the tone, it will, having someone like you working in the bar.'

In the morning light her surroundings appeared no better than they had yesterday. She made every effort to keep her skirts out of the filth, but her boots were sadly mired by the time she arrived at The Prince of Wales.

'Excuse me, sir, but I can't go in like this. Is there somewhere I can clean my boots?'

'We go round the back anyway; we've a decent yard where we store the empty barrels. You can use the pump out there. I'll fetch you a bit of rag.'

The alehouse didn't open until noon, so her work must be to clean up. After her experience this morning she thought she had the stomach to do anything without vomiting. Ma Peck was waiting impatiently.

'At last – make sure you're on time in future, my girl. Don't expect no mollycoddling from me. Remember you're on a week's trial.' Sarah curtsied and held her tongue. 'Here, put this over your gown. I want you looking smart when the bar opens.' Unexpectedly she smiled. 'Not that the rubbish that comes in here will appreciate the difference. I keep a clean house; no one gobs on my floor and gets away with it.'

The voluminous garment covered Sarah from head to foot. Obviously it had been worn by a far larger person. Fortunately her height meant it didn't trail on the floor. She was ready for whatever duties Mrs Peck might have. By the time she had removed the soiled sawdust from the floor, scrubbed the boards and sprinkled fresh, her hands were raw. Next the tables had to be scrubbed and polished and the wooden chairs wiped down.

By eleven thirty the place was spotless. However revolting the customers, this environment was preferable to her room. It smelled fresher and the winter sunlight streamed in through sparkling windows. There was a roaring fire to warm the room, and the smell of baking pasties and fresh bread drifted through from the kitchen. The outside cleaning was done by an old man, working for beer money and a hot meal.

'Right then, just got time for a bite to eat and a mug of tea before we start. You've done well, my girl. I'd not have thought you'd have it in you. When you've eaten, you need to put on one of the aprons hanging behind the door. I supply those – I like my girls to look smart.'

Sarah found it difficult to swallow, but free food was not to be turned down under any circumstances. By swallowing a mouthful of tea after each bite she managed to finish the pasty. The apron wrapped around her twice, but the ribbons kept it snug at her waist. Mr Peck had vanished as soon as he'd delivered her. Ma Peck had told her he was a carpenter by trade and had a workshop at The Hythe. Sarah wished his reassuring bulk was there when Ma Peck unbolted the doors at noon. The sound of stamping feet, raucous voices demanding to be let in – accompanied by such hacking, spitting and swearing – made her knees tremble. How was she going to cope serving beer to men like these?

4

Mrs Peck had told Sarah the prices of the other things she sold. These were hot pasties, pickles, and occasionally bread and cheese or beef sandwiches. However, this was only when there was a spare girl to make them. The Prince of Wales was generally quiet during the afternoon and early evening; the busy time was after the men returned from work, then the bar would be heaving.

The girls who worked at night were paid more than her, but Sarah was just grateful her employer had taken pity on her inexperience and given her the daytime shift. Walking back through the streets late, even though the main thoroughfares were lit by gas lamps, would be a terrifying experience. She wasn't used to the sort of people who lived round here, and having been brutally attacked in mid-afternoon she was well aware what desperate lengths the criminal classes would go to in order to obtain money.

'You ready, girl? Start filling the jugs. Have them ready for when the men come in. Take no notice of their foul mouths. Most mean no harm; they know no better.' She smiled thinly. 'You do your job properly and I'll look out for you, don't you worry.'

'I will, ma'am.'

The woman nodded and marched purposefully across the boards, her feet leaving imprints in the fresh sawdust. The door was unbolted and she stepped aside. Sarah had expected a press of rough men to charge in demanding their beer, but this was not the case. Mrs Peck stood by the door, arms folded, like a schoolmistress watching her pupils enter. The men touched their caps respectfully, and headed for the tables. There was an empty square in front of the hatch. No doubt this was filled with standing drinkers at busy times. The lunchtime crowd had more than enough seats and tables to go round.

As soon as they were safely inside they reverted to type; voices rose, hobnailed boots clattered, and complaints that she get a move on with their beer were loud and insistent. Ribald comments burned her ears. She kept her head down, knowing her cheeks were scarlet. She'd have to get used to this, become immune to the coarse remarks about the size of her backside, the fullness of her front and all the bits in between. Nod and smile, fill the tankards with the foaming liquid, and ignore the people she served. If she made no eye contact, with luck none of the men would attempt to take liberties with her person.

She carried three empty tankards in one hand and a full jug in the other. The men waiting to be served shouted encouragement, causing her to slop beer onto the floor. With shaking hand she placed a mug in front of the customers at the nearest table as she had been told to do, then carefully filled each up. The beer was tuppence a pint. The coins were slapped down on the table as she poured the beer.

She had a special pocket in the front of her apron that reached to her knees; in this she was to drop the coins. Keeping her face averted she murmured a soft thank you and moved on to the next group. Soon she was weaving in and out of the tables as if she'd been doing it all her life. A lot of the men reeked of stale sweat, but then they had been doing hard physical labour all morning. Some smelt downright foul, but at least half the customers were decent, hard-working men not much different from her stepfather.

After all it was Saturday – not every governor forced his employees to work that afternoon.

Men came and went. She ran back and forth to the barrels refilling her jug. Her feet were aching, her apron stained with beer and the pocket bulging with coppers. She'd have to ask where to put them; they were weighing her down and hampering her progress. How much longer did she have to work before her stint ended?

Mrs Peck had left most of the serving to her. She'd brought out the food and fetched down the pewter tankards for the regular customers. She also made sure the men kept their behaviour within acceptable bounds. There was a lull and she finally had time to ask about the money.

'I need to empty my pocket. I can't put any more in without bursting the seams.'

'Go into the kitchen. You'll see a metal strongbox on the table; empty it in there. Lock it and bring me the key.'

Sarah felt proud she'd been trusted with such a responsible task, having worked there only one day. She went into the kitchen hoping she'd meet Mr Peck, but the room was empty. All the pasties had gone, but the savoury smell lingered and her mouth watered. It was hours since she'd eaten.

It took her some time to empty the pocket. The heap of coins was most impressive; there could be more than a pound in the box. She closed the lid and turned the key. A slight movement alerted her. She looked round to see Mrs Peck had been watching her throughout the procedure. Her cheeks flushed; so much for thinking she was trusted.

The woman nodded, satisfied Sarah hadn't been dipping into the takings. She held out her hand for the key. 'Good girl, I can see I shan't have to keep such a sharp eye on you, not like some of the others. Most of the regulars have gone home to give what's left of their wages to their wives. Start clearing the mugs; you need to take them to the scullery and get them washed for this evening. You'll have to fetch water from the yard.'

'Yes, right away, Mrs Peck. Is there any particular order you want the tables clearing?'

'Get on with it, girl. Stop asking daft questions.'

Sarah decided the table furthest away from the hatch would be a sensible place to start, especially as it was unoccupied. The one adjacent had a solitary drinker. Stepping past him shouldn't be a problem.

'Excuse me, sir, I need to reach the empty mugs.' She waited for the man to drag his chair closer to the table. He looked up. She knew him; it was Mr Cooper. She'd never forget his shock of black hair and twinkling blue eyes gazing down at her as she lay injured on the pavement.

'I never expected to see *you* in The Prince of Wales, Miss Nightingale. Are you fully recovered? I don't suppose the constables got your money back for you or you wouldn't be working in a place like this.'

She glanced over her shoulder. It wouldn't do to be seen socialising with the customers, but Mrs Peck was absent, which allowed a few moments to converse. 'I'm quite well thank you, Mr Cooper. And I'm so glad to have seen you again. I wish to thank you for helping me. As you guessed, I didn't recover my savings and needless to say the perpetrators have not been apprehended either.'

'And this is the best you could find, I suppose?' His voice was deep, not rough-spoken like the others, and his eyes full of sympathy.

'I was left almost penniless, then I was turned out of my lodgings unexpectedly and obliged to find a room and employment or end up in the workhouse.' What had possessed her to tell a complete stranger such intimate details of her life? Her cheeks coloured and the empty tankards rattled in her hands. Something made her continue. 'Mr and Mrs Peck have been kind to me; I have a roof over my head and employment. *I'm* one of the fortunate ones, there are others far worse off than me in this neighbourhood.'

He smiled, his teeth white and even. She felt a strange flicker of something she did not recognise inside. 'I live at the bottom of Hythe Hill, but walk up here as this is the best alehouse in the area. Ma Peck keeps a decent establishment and a tight rein on her customers. You can get a quiet drink in this place without worrying if you'll be smashed on the head by a pot or a chair.'

Good God! She'd no idea that sort of thing went on in beerhouses. 'Excuse me, Mr Cooper, I must take the dirty pots. I'm to get them washed and ready for this evening's trade.'

'Do you work here after dark as well?'

She shook her head. 'No, I'm working the day shift only, but I'm on a week's trial. I daren't stand about talking any longer. Thank you again, sir, for your timely assistance the other week.'

Meeting Mr Cooper had brought back memories she'd much rather forget. It was a relief to busy herself in the scullery washing the stoneware tankards in the deep sink. The water was freezing, but at least she hadn't had to break the ice in order to do the washing-up. She left the mugs upside down on the draining board and then returned to the bar to collect the rest of the empties.

Occupied with this task she was excused further work in the public area. Apart from the fifteen minutes she'd sat down to consume her meal at half past eleven she'd been constantly on the go. She was used to long hours and hard work, but the scrubbing she'd done first thing had exhausted her. It wouldn't be right to ask when her shift ended but it had been dark for hours and must be getting on for six o'clock.

She was drying the last of the mugs when loud female voices echoed around the yard. Thank goodness, she could go home now. Without asking permission she stripped off her soiled apron and left it folded on the end of the draining board. The bead curtain that kept her employer's private quarters free from prying eyes also meant she could leave without hindrance.

Two young women not much older than her were in the kitchen tying on their aprons. Her words of greeting remained unspoken. These girls looked as bad as some of the customers; their clothes were sweat-stained and muddied around the hems, but their hair appeared free of lice and, from what she could see, they were clean enough. It was their faces that made the girls so different. They had a knowing look about them. These were not innocents, but experienced in the ways of the world. It was small wonder the girl she was replacing was off because she was in the family way.

The young women exchanged glances but didn't speak. 'Good evening, I'm Sarah. I can't tell you how glad I am to see you both. It's not that busy at the moment, and the tankards are done. I can't remember ever being so tired in my life before.'

The taller of the two, a blowsy blonde, shook her head in disbelief. 'Bloody hell! Where did Ma find you? You're not from round here, that's for sure. Would you look at her, Daisy!'

Daisy cackled, sounding more like an old woman than a girl in her prime. 'Hoity-toity! I reckon Ma has you working first because the regulars would eat yer alive at night. You get off, love – we'd not want the likes of you around when it gets busy.'

Hastily Sarah grabbed her cloak, but didn't say goodbye to her employer in case she was called back and asked to do something else. Daisy and the other girl were common but not vindictive, and seemed genuinely concerned for her welfare if she hung around much longer. She got paid less than they did and had been working almost ten hours. These two barmaids worked from six clock and would be finished by two in the morning. Maybe they had to work harder than she did, put up with more abuse and the groping hands of customers as they got inebriated.

She paused for a moment under the flickering gaslight, trying to remember her route home; everything was different in the dark. This would be the first time she'd tried to accomplish the journey to her lodgings on her own. She couldn't stand dawdling here; she had to get back before the streets were filled with riff-raff. Pulling her cloak tight she rushed round the corner to collide with a solid object. She stumbled backwards, almost falling, but two strong arms shot out and grasped her elbows to steady her.

'Take care, miss, you don't want to fall over.'

She was relieved to find it was Mr Cooper coming to her rescue a second time. 'I thought you left some time ago. I'm sorry to have bumped into you. I wasn't watching where I was going.'

'I waited. I'll walk with you. A young lady like you shouldn't be out alone in the dark – not round here. I can't think what Ma's thinking of, letting you walk home by yourself.'

'Mr Cooper, I thank you for your concern, but I'm quite capable of getting myself home safely. It's neither your nor my employer's responsibility. I bid you good evening.'

He was clearly not offended by her rebuff, as the rich, warm sound of his laughter filled the darkness. 'You're not in the High Street now, miss. Things are different round here. Being polite won't stop you being attacked. I'd have thought what happened to you a while ago would have taught you that.'

There was the sound of rough voices approaching. Four unkempt men

swaggered down the pathway. Suddenly she was lifted to one side, Mr
Cooper placing his bulk between her and them. She liked the feel of his
tweed coat up against her cheek – she remembered his smell of wood
shavings and tobacco. They passed with no more than a few vulgar
comments. God knows what would have happened to her if she'd been
unprotected.

'Come along, miss, the sooner you're off the streets the better. Here,
take my arm. I'll be happier knowing you're by my side.'

Why was he taking such an interest? A handsome man like him, in his
mid-twenties, must be married with a family of his own to worry about.
Maybe his interest was neighbourly, but she couldn't take the risk. She'd
not get involved with a married man, not for all the tea in China.

'Do you have children, Mr Cooper? I used to be a nurse at a big house
on East Hill; I love looking after little ones, but as I was obliged to leave
without references, I must do whatever I can to avoid the workhouse.'

He ignored the last part of her speech. 'I have three boys, little rascals,
but I'm that proud of them. There's another expected next spring. Maria,
my wife, is hoping for a girl this time. I'm not bothered either way, but if
that's what she wants, then for her sake I hope it's a girl.'

She was obviously mistaken; she had no experience of men – married
or otherwise. He adored his family, loved his wife and was just being
gallant. It must be pleasant being married to such a man. His wife was a
lucky woman to have a husband who was not only attractive but also had
regular work, a home of his own and was prepared to help those less
fortunate than himself.

'Mrs Cooper must be wondering where you are; your boys will be
wanting to see their father. I won't hold you up. Thank you for bringing
me this far.'

He shook his head. 'I'll take you to your door. It's the back alleys that
are the worst. You can't see where you're going, and anyone could be lurk-
ing, waiting to rob you. I know you don't have much, but a few pennies
will buy a quart of ale. The beerhouses will be filling up, the men coming
home with their wages. You don't want to be around on your own right
now. Buy yourself a lantern with your first wages.'

The street lighting didn't stretch between the dilapidated buildings.

The new gas lights only ran down the main thoroughfare. Light from these was enough for them to see the first few yards, but after that it was anybody's guess what they were walking in. She directed him down the next walk and pointed to the door of the end house.

'This is where I live; I'll be quite safe now. I have to learn to manage on my own, Mr Cooper. I cannot expect strangers to walk me home every night. I thank you for your kindness.'

'I hope you don't consider me a stranger. You know my name, and I know yours. Sarah Nightingale's a pretty name – it suits you. I shall be having a word with Ma next time I'm in. I shall ask her to get John to see you home safe.'

She let herself into her lodgings. It was scarcely warmer in the passage than it was outside. She was so tired, she'd not bother to light the fire or make herself a hot drink. She'd go straight to bed. It was cheaper being under the covers than sitting around with the fire lit. It was so cold she decided to sleep in her clothes, piling her cloak on top of the thin blankets to keep warm.

Teeth chattering, she abandoned the idea and scrambled out of bed to light the fire after all. She was too soft for this sort of life. She'd not survive the deprivation unless she toughened up. Once she was nursing a mug of tea in front of the fire she began to feel more optimistic. The room wasn't so bad, the job bearable; if she could just think of a way to get herself home after work then she'd be fine.

5

COLCHESTER, DECEMBER 1843

Sarah had no time to think about her reduced circumstances. As Christmas approached even the afternoons were busy at The Prince of Wales. She was rushed off her feet most days and returned too exhausted to bother to eat a hot meal. Each night one of the customers was waiting to escort her home, Dan Cooper had spread the word around amongst the decent men who frequented the alehouse. Some family men, others unwed, but all happy to walk back with her when she finished her shift. She got to know each of her guards and through them had met one or two wives and daughters.

Her life was no longer lonely; she couldn't invite anyone back to her slum on a Sunday, which after her week's trial became her day off. Occasionally she was invited to visit one of these new friends for tea. Sometimes she considered sending a message to Betty. She missed her, and she'd like to let her know she'd found somewhere to live and wasn't on the streets. However, she couldn't bear to think of everyone at Grey Friars House knowing how far she'd slipped since she'd left there. No, it was better that they remembered her how she used to be, smart and tidy, well-behaved and a credit to her employers.

Dan Cooper walked her back on a Saturday night, which was the only day he allowed himself the luxury of a few drinks. His family seemed more familiar than her own; Joe was seven, Davie six and John three. Maria and Dan had been married eight years. They'd been only seventeen when they let their love get the better of them and had been forced to marry in haste. From the way Mr Cooper spoke of his wife it was definitely not a case of their repenting at leisure. He loved her, and his three boys, but she detected a note of anxiety in his voice when he spoke about the current pregnancy. Maria was not as hale as she had been with the other three, was tiring easily, and in spite of having a woman in to do the heavy work was finding it difficult to take care of her three lively boys.

The weather took a turn for the worse and tramping backwards and forwards from The Prince of Wales ankle-deep in snow did nothing to improve Sarah's enjoyment of her job. She'd become a firm favourite with many customers. Even the drunks and ne'er-do-wells treated her with a modicum of respect. She still worked the day shift, but she was now getting the same amount as the other two girls.

Daisy and Josie were loud and vulgar but kind-hearted, not the sort of girls she'd have chosen to be friends with. They looked out for her, warned her about the regulars who would try and short-change her or would take a crafty grope under her skirts when she was bending down to serve another customer.

Sarah had expected to be given Christmas Day off, that at least on the Lord's birthday Ma Peck would show some respect and keep her establishment closed.

'Close on Christmas Day? I should think not, Sarah. It's one of the busiest days of the year – that and New Year. The men don't have to go to work and the women want them out from under their feet, especially if they got the wherewithal to cook a special meal.'

'I'd hoped I could go to church, Mrs Peck. I've never missed attending on Christmas Day since I can remember.'

'Ain't there an early service? You can go to that before you come, my girl. I can't say fairer than that. I won't dock your wages neither – call it your Christmas box.'

Sarah tried to look happy. 'Ta, that's very generous of you. I believe there's a service at eight o'clock, which means I can be here a little after nine. Does anything different happen on Christmas Day? Do you roast chestnuts or serve mulled wine or something like that?'

Mr Peck walked into the kitchen and overheard her suggestion. 'Well Ma, what do you think? Roasting chestnuts and a hot toddy? That would bring the punters in and no mistake. You've always said you've got a better class in here. I've noticed, certainly of an afternoon, that things are quieter and more genteel.' He beamed at Sarah, who paused for a moment with her tasks. 'My dear, you've brought a bit of class to the place and that's for sure.'

Ma wasn't best pleased by this remark. As far as she was concerned her bar was a cut above the rest anyway. 'Get about your work, Sarah. I don't pay you to stand around talking.'

Sarah curtsied briefly, then dashed back to collect the bucket of clean sawdust and scatter it on the freshly scrubbed floorboards. This was a job she enjoyed. It meant the drudgery was over. When it was done she could sit down with mug of tea, a hot pasty and a slice of bread and cheese.

The only day for shopping was on Sunday; fortunately shops were open from first thing in the morning until eleven o'clock. Some men didn't come out of the pub until closing time on Saturdays, and *their* womenfolk didn't get their housekeeping money until they staggered back. If the shops weren't open, families would have gone without their Sunday dinner.

Her clothes hung from her. Not being able to cook in her room was a major handicap to good health. Being provided with a decent meal at midday was not enough to prevent her losing weight. She'd given up eating breakfast and only occasionally bought herself fried fish or a hot meat pie for supper.

She thought longingly of the food she'd been given whilst working at Grey Friars. What she wouldn't give for a plate of Cook's tasty mutton stew. Strangely the image of her little brother Tommy had faded. It was Alfie she wanted to see; it was he she kept close to her heart in the hope that one day he would walk into The Prince of Wales and take her away from this miserable life. Her brief conversations with Dan Cooper, hearing about his happy family, just made her miss her brother more.

Attending church on Christmas Day meant she had to be ready earlier than usual. It was unpleasant trudging through the slush; the snow was thawing and the pathways were even more treacherous. This morning was the first time since she'd been making this journey that the shops were shuttered, few folk about, and she was able to reach the haven of St Leonard's Church without being accosted.

She was a regular there, but being a poor working girl could no longer sit, and must remain standing in the empty space at the back throughout the service. It was colder inside the ancient building than it was outside. Instead of thinking joyous thoughts, it was all she could do to stop her fingers turning blue and her teeth rattling in between the droning from the vicar and the congregation's responses. Thank God there were no hymns to sing. The sooner she could get to work and warm up the better.

The reverend gentleman galloped through the service, obviously as eager to get away to his vicarage as she was to leave. She arrived at The Prince of Wales, for the first time pleased to be there. As she stepped in through the kitchen door the heavenly smell of roasting chestnuts greeted her. Good heavens! Why were they doing these now? The doors didn't open until midday; the chestnuts would be shrivelled and ruined by then.

She hung her cloak on its customary peg and picked up her overall. Mr Peck appeared carrying a basket. 'Happy Christmas, my dear girl. Sit yourself down. Ma and I intend for you to share a festive breakfast with us today. See, I have here the chestnuts you suggested. I bought a sack at the produce market last Wednesday. We're going to offer them to the customers when they come in, for a halfpenny a plate.'

Ma Peck appeared from the bar and Sarah looked at her nervously. This was so out of character. She didn't like to be idle when she would normally be working.

'Sit down, girl, before I change my mind. Now, I've got boiled eggs, hot muffins, and fresh beef dripping for the toast. It will be a feast, and to finish we'll have the chestnuts. I reckon they'll be cool enough by then.'

This was the first time since leaving Ada's house that Sarah was so full she couldn't eat another morsel. She licked her fingers, sighing. 'I can't tell you how much I enjoyed that breakfast. That was the best present I've ever had in my whole life.' She blinked furiously. 'I know I'm not the sort of girl you usually employ, but you gave me a chance and I hope I've not let you down.'

Mr Peck banged on the table making the crockery jump. 'I should say not, my dear. Word is spreading you know. It started with Dan Cooper coming up the hill because he liked a place he could drink without getting his head bashed in. He spread the word, and others followed. Still a bit rough on Saturday night, but the rest of the time it's a respectable place.' He beamed at her.

'We're thinking of turning the kitchen and scullery into a saloon and catering for those with more money to spend. Dan Cooper has suggested we have a savings club in here, somewhere a workingman can put his money of a Saturday before he's spent it all on beer.'

'I'm sure that will be much appreciated. I'd like to put a few pennies a week away in a savings club. I had all my money stolen from me when I took it out of the bank.'

The two exchanged glances. 'We thought as much. You're a hard worker and the customers like you. Your misfortune was our gain.'

Sarah cleared away the debris from the table. She wasn't going to outstay her welcome. It might be Christmas Day but there was still a floor to scrub and tables to do. They wouldn't polish themselves. Whilst scrubbing, she began to wish she'd eaten rather less, but having a full stomach was worth the discomfort. She had more energy than usual this morning. The aroma of hot chestnuts filled the room with a festive feel and this mingled with the apple logs bought specially for today. The tobacco smoke and the smell of unwashed bodies was less evident. She could almost believe the bar was already catering for the middling folk instead of rough workmen.

It was a pity that Mrs Peck had not wanted pitchers of mulled wine standing around the fire as she could have done with a drink to help her keep going. Daisy and Josie had the day off. The Prince of Wales was closing when her shift ended. All very well for them, but it meant she had to wait until the last customer left as she had to wash all the tankards up before she could go.

An elderly man remained behind. 'I'll hang on for you, love; I'm walking your way. You don't want anything to spoil your day.'

'That's very kind of you, Mr Davies. I'll be as quick as I can. You sit by the fire; there'll be a fair old draught as I'm going in and out to the scullery.'

Her employers had already retired upstairs, leaving her to finish on her own. They'd taken the strongbox with them, so that was one less thing to worry about. She was to call when she'd done, and Mr Peck would come down and lock up after her. Tonight she was to leave by the front door; the yard and kitchen were already bolted for the night.

It was nearer seven when she eventually stepped out into the crisp night air. 'Would you look at that, Mr Davies, a carpet of stars up there! I wonder which one is the star that the three wise men were supposed to have followed.'

'I don't reckon it's one of those, love. It were nigh on two thousand years ago. It was sent just to guide them and the shepherds. What would we want with a guiding star now?' He struggled to button up his coat, his gnarled fingers refusing to obey. Her interference would not be appreciated. Eventually he managed one and then wrapped his muffler tightly around his neck and tucked the ends in to cover the gap. Pulling his cap on firmly he held out his arm.

'Here, take my arm. We can hold each other up. This pavement's sheet ice, and we'll be on our arses if we're not careful.'

Tom Davies had no children at home. He'd told her one son had taken the Queen's shilling; the other was at sea. He lived in a tiny cottage with his wife a couple of hundred yards from the turning she took to her lodging house. 'I hope Mrs Davies will not be put out because you waited for me.'

'Bless you, child, she was glad to see the back of me. It was she suggested I go for a pint and walk you home. I'm to ask you to come back with me, if you'd care to, and share a cold collation with us.'

'I would love to. How kind of you to think of me. I was dreading going back to my room.'

'Well, that's grand. The missus has been saying ever since I mentioned you starting that she's eager to meet you and hear how a nice girl like you ended up round here with the likes of us.'

'It's the usual story, Mr Davies, but I shall be happy to share it if you really want to know. I seem to remember you live not far from me.'

'That's right, my dear, you'll only have a few hundred yards to go back. We're almost neighbours, ain't we?'

'At least I didn't have to light my lantern this evening. The moon makes things as bright as day.'

One of the first things she'd purchased, at Mr Cooper's insistence, was a small lantern. This made the last part of her journey less hazardous as she could see where she was putting her feet. The stinking alleys were no longer such a nightmare, the light seeming to scare the rats away. Occasionally she saw shadowy faces peering out at her from doorways but so far no one had stepped forward to molest her.

Apart from the drunks this wasn't such a bad area. The inhabitants were almost destitute, their children neglected and barefoot, but most wished her no harm. She'd not heard of any girls being raped or of anyone being murdered. Maybe she was worrying unnecessarily.

'Here we are, love, home sweet home.' Mr Davies knocked loudly and the door was pulled open. A wave of heat welcomed them.

A tiny lady, her face so wrinkled it had the appearance of a prune, drew her inside. 'There you are, Tom. I have supper waiting for us in front of the fire. Come in, my dear, it's not often we get a visitor.'

They stepped directly into the room. It had proper boards on the floor, a generous fireplace and two comfortable armchairs either side. As she removed her cloak and bonnet, Mrs Davies slammed the door and pulled across a thick curtain. It was cosy and made her realise just how much her own room lacked.

She spent a pleasant hour or so in the cottage and when she rose to leave, Mrs Davies insisted on wrapping up what was left of the supper for her to take back with her. Several slices of cold meat, a piece of plum cake and some freshly baked bread all went into a small basket.

'Drop the basket back on Sunday when you have your day off, Sarah love. I'll have a nice tea ready for you and plenty for you to take home.'

On impulse Sarah leant forward and gave the old lady a hug. 'I have really enjoyed myself, Mrs Davies, and I should love to come to tea next

Sunday.' The old couple reminded her of her grandparents in West Bergholt. How long would it be before she could see them again?

Mr Davies had fallen asleep in his chair half an hour since and Sarah decided it would be unfair to make him go out again. It was only a few hundred yards back to her room; she'd be there in no time.

The sound of the bolts being pushed across the door behind her made her feel more alone than she had for weeks. It was getting on for nine o'clock. The sound of revellers celebrating came from various beerhouses close by. She shivered. Rough men were flocking from the alleys and cuts, heading for the beerhouses.

There were so many, some little more than a room at the front of a cottage. To be a proprietor the tenants merely had to have enough to buy the licence. Mrs Peck had said there was no restriction on the where-abouts or facilities of these places. There must be half a dozen at least within a stone's throw of where she was standing and all of them filled with men she'd rather avoid.

This was the first time she'd been out on her own so late. Why hadn't she made a move earlier, when the streets were quieter, the hostelries less raucous? This was ridiculous. It was not far to her turning and the pathway was lit by gas lamps. All she had to do was negotiate the dark areas between the lamps safely. Wasn't that why she'd bought the lantern in the first place? She wished the moon had stayed out just a little longer.

It was dark here, the next pool of light fifty yards ahead, and then it was her turning next. The sound of breaking glass and raised voices from the establishment over the road made her set off briskly. Unsteady foot-steps behind her warned her that a group of inebriated men were approaching.

She melted into the shadows letting the group walk by, positive she hadn't been spotted; she'd been most careful to keep her lantern within the folds of her cloak. The sooner she got home the better. It might be Christmas Day, but those three men were full of the wrong sort of Christmas spirit.

Over the weeks she'd developed her own way of walking fast, but not running which would draw attention to herself. Only tonight she had a basket of food over one arm and was obliged to hold up her skirts with the same hand. This was awkward as the path was slippery. She was concentrating on remaining upright and not paying attention to the men in front.

Before she realised it they had stopped. She was surrounded, one behind and two in front. They'd chosen the spot carefully. It was dark; the light from the two gas lamps didn't reach this far.

'Look here, Bill, it's that pretty little girl what works at The Prince of Wales. Never has a kind word to say to the likes of us.'

The speaker moved closer. She wanted to step away, but if she did she would be pressed up against his equally repellent companion. The stink from the three of them made her gag; she felt her stomach lurching. She prayed she wouldn't vomit over their boots.

'Well then, where's your fancy man now to protect you? I bet you spread your legs quick enough for him of a Saturday night.' A groping hand cupped her backside and started pulling up her skirts.

Bill, the man to her right, reached out and touched her cheek with his rancid finger. 'Who's having her first then? Grab hold of her, Freddie boy, put yer hand over her gob. We'll take the stuck-up bitch down the alley. Nobody will bother us there.'

There was no point in screaming; her cries would go unnoticed in the row coming from the beerhouses nearby. Gripping her basket firmly in one hand and her lantern in the other, she readied herself. She was trapped between them. Their filthy hands would soon be on her body. She'd been robbed and evicted but she was damned if she was going to be raped on Christmas Day.

From somewhere came a rage, a surge of madness that gave her the courage to act. She swung the lantern back and smashed it into the face of the man in front. The glass broke, the oil spilled, and suddenly her attacker was on fire, his muffler and jacket ablaze.

Snatching her skirts from the ground she took to her heels, praying it would take the man's companions several minutes to beat out the fire. She hoped it looked worse than it was, that the small amount of oil would not do serious damage.

She skidded round her turning, not pausing to catch her breath, the sound of her pursuers growing closer. It was pitch-dark at the end of this alley, but she'd made this journey so many times she would have an advantage over those brutes. Almost there. Turn right, then the length of the walk between the overhanging houses and she would be safe. She ran pell-mell to her front door, thanking God Mr Peck had rehung it and it opened and closed without the need of a hefty shoulder.

At any second they could appear at the corner. She had to be inside before they saw which house she lived in. She pushed the door shut, not banging it – the sound would echo in the night. On tiptoes she crept to her room, key ready in her hand. It took several attempts to turn it, her fingers refusing to allow her to insert it in the lock.

Finally it turned. She fell into her sanctuary. The bolt was across – she'd escaped. She was safe. Her breathing ragged, she waited in the freezing darkness. Would the rapists have seen where she lived? Coarse male voices shouting in the street made her legs buckle. She could do no more. She drew her knees up under her chin, and huddled, as she had in the candle cupboard at Grey Friars House all that while ago.

6

The sound of mice scratching behind the wall and the occasional thump and shout from another tenant were the only sounds in the darkness. Sarah had no idea how long she'd been cowering on the damp floor praying to a God she wasn't sure existed. Well, the men had gone, so perhaps her prayers had been answered.

She inched her way up the door until she was standing. With her eyes open there was enough moonlight filtering in through the window for her to move around freely in the freezing darkness. She needed a fire; she was chilled to the marrow. The warmth and cheerfulness of a blaze might help restore her.

Her tinderbox was resting on the shelf. She'd seen men using the new lucifers – the little stick with its phosphorescent head bursting into flames when struck against a rough surface. They were expensive, but maybe when she was settled she'd invest in a small box. It would certainly make life easier. Having to fiddle around striking a flint onto a bit of fluff was tiresome and all but impossible when your hands were so cold they weren't working properly.

With the fire finally lit, her pan balanced precariously over the flames, the room was warm enough to risk removing her cloak. She draped it over the table hoping it would be dry by the time she wanted to spread it across the bed. Lighting a second candle was extravagant, but one wasn't sufficient tonight. Anyway, it was the Lord's birthday, a time of celebration and rejoicing, although she didn't feel much like doing either at the moment.

It was fortunate, certainly, that she'd escaped from her encounter with no worse than a scare and a lost lantern. But those men would not forget what she'd done; they didn't know her exact address but they had followed her to the walk outside. She'd heard them shouting. How long would it take for them to discover the exact house? They could be waiting for her tomorrow night, break in and rape her and then slit her throat.

There was no option; she'd have to find herself a position in a different part of town, fresh lodgings, make another life for herself. She'd only been working at The Prince of Wales for a few weeks. Her employers had been kind to her and it wouldn't look good leaving so abruptly. Mrs Peck might not give her a reference, and she'd not find work so easily a second time without one. Writing her own reference was not an option any more – the cost of the materials was beyond her meagre resources.

She wouldn't be sorry to leave this room, but it was cheap and she'd managed to add a few coins to her savings every Saturday. Whilst she waited for the water to boil she reached under her pillow and withdrew her purse; there was a satisfying clunk as she shook the contents onto the table.

She counted it most nights. It gave her the reassurance she needed that her savings were growing and not shrinking. Occasionally an extra farthing or halfpenny was left on the table; at first she'd not known what to do with it, but Daisy had told her it was hers. Some regulars liked to reward a barmaid for good service. As long as they didn't expect favours in return she was happy to drop it into her skirt pocket.

These coins, and her frugal diet, meant her wages were more than adequate to live on. She balanced the last penny on the pile; there was almost two pounds. Not a fortune, but surely enough to keep her from destitution until she found employment elsewhere. Next time she hoped to afford a more salubrious lodging; it might be better not to inform Mrs Peck she was giving in her notice until she'd done so.

She didn't enjoy bar work, but she'd come to like her employers, especially Mr Peck. Perhaps he'd give her a reference and she could find herself a job in a better class of hostelry. A big place like The Cups or The Red Lion would be ideal. There might be board and lodging included at a coaching inn, which would solve the problem of finding suitable accommodation.

She shuddered, remembering the red-faced, loud farmers who had packed out the bar the day she'd gone into The Red Lion with Betty. She'd hated the way some of the customers deliberately brushed against her as they passed, made lewd suggestions, leered at her over the top of their tankards. She wasn't *that* sort of girl. The very thought of one of those men touching her filled her with disgust. It might well be even worse with middling folk. They thought themselves better than those less fortunate and they might believe that they were entitled to take liberties.

The girls she worked with had been talking about Mary, the one she'd replaced. As soon as the baby was born it would be given up. The unfortunate girl was already within the confines of the workhouse. Daisy had assured her Mary hadn't been casual with her affections; the young man concerned had promised her a cottage and a ring on her finger before she'd agreed. As soon as she'd caught on he'd vanished, leaving her to throw herself on the parish.

A handsome face and a winning smile would not make *her* forget how to behave. And even if a girl got wed, a constant stream of babies would surely follow. Look at Ada Billings – she was worn down by all the children she had borne. She hoped her friend was managing without her; she hadn't liked the look of that Mr Billings. He didn't seem the sort of man to offer his wife any assistance.

The tea was black, but she'd become used to this; milk and sugar were luxuries she couldn't afford. The rustling above her head reminded her of the basket of food Mrs Davies had given her. She was amazed she hadn't dropped it during her flight. It couldn't be left where it was – the mice she could hear scampering in the ceiling would devour it whilst she was in bed.

There was never any food left over. She bought just enough to feed her after work and had stopped eating breakfast altogether so this was the first time she'd been faced with this problem.

Collecting the basket, she removed the folded napkin and placed it on the table. Inside were three slices of ham, a wedge of cheese and a twist of paper in which were three pickled onions. She was tempted to eat it straight away, not risk her nocturnal visitors getting it first. However, her stomach was more full of food than it had been in weeks; she couldn't force another morsel down.

In a separate package was a generous slice of plum cake and a piece of apple tart. It was sufficient to last her for several days if somehow she could protect it. There'd not been droppings on the shelf so this must be the safest place in the room. She removed her clean petticoat from inside the pillowslip and wrapped it several times around the food and then replaced the bundle in the basket.

Tomorrow was a normal working day so she'd better get herself into bed. She smiled and stretched contentedly. The room was warm enough to remove her outer garments without turning blue; in fact she could put on her nightgown. The thought of being so vulnerable made her decide to leave it where it was, inside the pillowslip.

As usual it was her drawers and petticoats. She grinned as she snuggled down beneath the blankets, recalling something Daisy had told her. Her mother had used to sew the unfortunate girl into her undergarments for the winter. It didn't bear thinking of; her childhood had been luxurious compared to those she worked with now. Although it was impossible to wash her gowns, her underclothes and stockings were clean and she regularly rinsed the hems and scrubbed the sweat stains from the armpits of her two dresses.

Sarah had expected to lie awake, but she slept well, the warmth of the room making her relax. She woke suddenly, not sure what had disturbed her. She'd been deep in a nightmare, standing at the head of a flight of stairs whilst her brother had been climbing towards her. But the faster he ran more stairs appeared in front of him. It was a relief to be awake.

It was dark, but the small square of moonlight from the high window gave sufficient light to see. The house was quiet, not even a child wailing in the darkness. Something had woken her. Then she heard the scrabbling above her head. The mice had discovered her food and were having a festive feast of their own.

She scrambled out of bed to snatch the basket from the shelf, holding it at arm's length, not sure what she should do next. Determined to save some of the food, but loath to have the livestock in the basket tumble out over her bare feet, she gingerly stretched out and placed the object on the table.

The scrabbling had stopped. It was ominously silent. She would take them outside, but first she must put on her boots and cloak. Hopefully, if she upturned the basket the rodents would fall out and what was left of her food would remain behind. The petticoat would have to be washed; she didn't fancy wearing it when the mice had made free with it all night.

In unlaced boots, her cloak securely clasped around her neck, she grasped the basket handle and carried it from the room, having unbolted the door already. Leaving the door ajar – she wasn't going to be gone more than a few moments – she stepped out into the freezing darkness of the narrow passageway.

It was a struggle opening the back door one-handed but eventually she was outside. Placing the basket on the ground she pushed it sideways with the poker she'd had the forethought to bring with her. Three small grey shapes tumbled out and vanished. She straightened the basket, prodding it a few times to see if anything else jumped out.

Satisfied the livestock had abandoned their meal she hooked the handle over the poker and carried it back into her room. She rattled the basket a few more times until she was satisfied the mice had gone. The ham and cheese were untouched; however, the mice had made severe inroads into the plum cake and apple pie. She was tempted to throw it all away but this would be a disgraceful waste. She couldn't bring herself to eat it. She had not been living in penury long enough to lose her own fastidiousness, but there were children starving in the street who would think this a feast.

She removed each item, shaking off any droppings, then cut away the nibbled pieces. She rewrapped what was left in the napkin and put it back in the basket. No doubt the mice were already making their way back into the house. There was no point in leaving the food in the room – she would take it with her and give it away.

Dealing with the mice pushed her attack to the back of her mind, and when she set off for work hoping to find recipients for her bounty, she quite forgot to check if she was being followed. It was so early there were no children abroad; she'd have to find someone on her return. Laughing she explained to Mrs Peck what had happened with the mice.

'Put it in the pantry. My tomcat makes sure we have no mice in here. You want to get yourself a cat; they don't cost much to feed and it would be company of a night.'

'I'll think about it, Mrs Peck. I'll get on with the floor. There'll be chestnut peelings all over it this morning.'

She was so busy, what had happened the previous night was all but forgotten. There were chestnuts to roast and serve, and the bar was full. She got a few peculiar looks but didn't take any notice; however, when two of the less pleasant customers snarled at her she was forced to admit things had changed.

She tried to avoid the corner of the room where these two sat. They didn't have the wherewithal to order a refill, thank goodness. Mr Cooper came towards the end of her shift; she felt safe now he was there, nobody would take liberties with him about. The width of his shoulders, the strength of his fists and the steely glint in his eye would discourage all but the most determined.

The bar was quiet, everyone gone, apart from one or two dozing by the fire reluctant to return to their cold lodgings. Dan Cooper, as always, was last to go. He waited for her to finish so he could walk her home. He beckoned her over. Sarah checked that Mrs Peck was elsewhere. 'Sit down a minute, Sarah. I need to talk to you.' She sat and waited. He grinned. 'I've been hearing all about you, that you set fire to Fred Paterson last night. Is it true?'

The way he described it, it seemed funny, and she returned his smile. 'Three men stopped me. They said they were going to...' Her cheeks flushed scarlet.

His smile vanished. 'Did they indeed. We'll see about that. It's not safe for you around here any more. My Maria has been asking me to persuade you to come and work for us. Ever since I told her you were a trained nursemaid she's not let up. I didn't think it a good idea, but now things are different.'

'Mr Cooper, are you offering me employment? Will I be living in?'

He nodded. He didn't appear too keen on the idea – perhaps employing a girl without references worried him. 'I can't pay much mind, but you'll get board and lodging and you'll be safe under my roof. There's a woman comes in to do the heavy work; you'll take care of the boys and do the cooking.'

She couldn't believe she'd been given such a wonderful opportunity. 'I promise you'll not regret this, Mr Cooper. I don't eat much and I'll do the heavy work as well. You can give me what you gave her.'

He frowned, shaking his head. 'I'm not putting someone out of work; the money she earns keeps her off the parish.'

She hung her head; she hadn't meant to offend him. 'I beg your pardon, Mr Cooper. I meant no harm by the suggestion.'

'Good, that's settled. The sooner you're out of that room the better. I've spoken to Ma Peck and she's in agreement. You're not safe here any more. John Peck will come with us. He's bringing a handcart for your belongings. Your room will be the attic. It ain't big, but it's clean and dry, and warmed by the chimney breast that runs through it. Anything you've got by way of furniture of your own will be helpful.'

She wanted to reach out and shake his hand, to embrace him, but he didn't look the sort of man who'd take kindly to such a gesture. She detected he was only taking her on to please his wife, that if she hadn't been in such a perilous position he would never have spoken. Betty had been wrong; Dan Cooper certainly hadn't taken a shine to her. Indeed, he seemed most reluctant to take her on.

'I thank you, sir; I'd already decided to start looking for employment elsewhere. I never thought things would fall into place like this. I won't let you and Mrs Cooper down. I love children, and I can read and write. I'd be happy to teach them their letters if you wish me to.'

'My older boys already attend infant school most mornings so that won't be necessary. Now get a move on, the sooner we get your things the quicker I'll be home to my family.'

Flanked by two substantial men, Sarah was in no danger from anyone. Mr Peck had a lantern tied to his cart, and using this they were able to find their way to the front door of her lodgings without mishap. She led the way, belatedly remembering she had her damp petticoat draped across the table. Too late to worry about such niceties. She unlocked the door, stepping in front of them in order to snatch up the offending garment and toss it on the bed.

'Bugger me! I can't believe you've been living in this rathole all these weeks, Sarah, and still turning up at work cheerful and smart.'

'It's all I could afford, Mr Cooper. As you can imagine, I shan't be sorry to leave.'

He chuckled. 'Compared to this, the room you'll have will seem like luxury.'

In little less than half an hour they were retracing their steps, she still clutching the basket of food. When would she have time to return it to Mrs Davies? She'd been invited to tea next Sunday. 'Mr Cooper, I went to visit with Mr and Mrs Davies last night. It was on the way back from their cottage that I was attacked. She's invited me to tea next Sunday when I'm to return this basket.'

His brow creased. 'I ain't a hard taskmaster, Sarah, but you're not to come up here again, even to return a basket. I'll give it to him when I see him next. He'll understand when I explain the circumstances.' His voice was abrupt. She felt rebuffed and less certain of her welcome in his house.

A group of ragged children were watching wide-eyed as they passed. Quickly she removed the food and held it out to the largest. 'Would you like this? There's ham and cheese and a few other things as well.'

He didn't need asking twice; the urchin clutched the bundle to his chest. He was not much more than five years old, and he grinned. With his siblings beside him he raced back into the alleyway; she hoped the children would all get a fair share of the food.

She had two pounds in her purse and was to work with children again. This was the second time she had somehow managed to avoid disaster. It was nothing short of miraculous. As they trundled past St Leonard's Church she closed her eyes and sent up a prayer of thanks. She'd never doubt the existence of the Lord again.

7

LONDON, JANUARY 1844

More than two years had passed since he'd left home and Alfie no longer thought about returning to Colchester. He'd built up a steady business and sometimes employed an extra boy to push the third cart. He and Jim had replaced the money they'd spent and there was a small fortune put by to rent themselves a cottage with a yard sometime in the spring.

He stayed away from Bishopsgate and had all but forgotten he'd ever belonged to a gang of thieves. Jim was thriving; he was taller and had filled out a treat. George Benson from upstairs had become a good friend as well. He'd been learning him how to use the carpentry tools of a Sunday and Alfie reckoned he was a natural. They might even suggest to George that they shared a yard. It made good sense.

After the holiday season things wasn't as busy, but there was a steady trickle of business, and if they had to go further afield to find it, then so what? They was fit and healthy and the more they worked the more they had to put in their savings. Alfie was tempted to stick it in one of them savings clubs he'd heard about. The Pig and Whistle, his local hostelry, ran such a thing. The weather was foul. More ice, snow and sleet plagued them until the middle of January. Even with thick coats, extra socks to wear inside their boots, and gloves on their hands they were near frozen to death.

Alfie no longer looked over his shoulder. It was eighteen months since they'd split away from the gang and something would have happened before this. Jim was confident enough to work on his own. Sometimes Alfie sent Buster, but the dog preferred to remain at his side. When the weather was inclement the animal had to be persuaded to leave his warm spot on the rug in front of the fire.

He couldn't credit that this huge, friendly dog was the same vicious tyke what had spent the first few years of his life living on a coal barge. The snow thawed but was replaced by a bitter east wind, and Jim developed a hacking cough. Alfie decided it wouldn't hurt for both of them to take the day off. They had nothing booked until the following week; why not stay in the warm and toast crumpets in front of the fire?

'You know, Jim, I've been living in London almost two years and you're the only friend I got apart from George and Buster. The man on the coal lighter I ran away from, that bastard Black Ben, he'd slit my throat, or do me in with a shovel, if he got the chance. I reckon Ginger and the others from our old gang would do the same, and Silas the fence would be right behind them. I seem to have a knack of making enemies not friends.'

Jim was coughing so hard he couldn't answer. Alfie handed him a mug of tea. 'Thanks, Alfie. My chest feels as if someone's sitting on it. I don't reckon I'll be well enough to work tomorrow. I'm right poorly and no mistake.'

'You don't have to work, not if you're ill. We've done so well this past year we can afford to take it easy. You stop in the warm; I'll go to Finsbury Market on me own. Pity to miss the chance of making a few bob.'

'You'd better take the dog. I'll be fine here. Buster could do with the exercise; he's getting right lazy nowadays. How old is he, do you know?'

'Ain't the faintest idea, but he must be five or six. You hear that, Buster? You're coming with me tomorrow. Jim's stopping here in the warm for a change.'

Several times he was woken by Jim's coughing. If his friend were no better in a couple of days he'd have to find a quack. He'd try some cough syrup first; he'd get it on the way home tomorrow. He crept off the next morning without waking his friend who had finally fallen into a restless sleep an hour or two before dawn.

The market was poorly attended; most folk must have thought it better to stay at home than come out in this weather. He got two deliveries and made two shillings, enough to spend on medicine for Jim. He jogged the last mile; he couldn't feel his fingers or toes but the thought of a warm room and a hot mug of tea drove him on. Buster was limping at his side looking sorry for himself.

The wheels banged and rattled on the cobbles. He was too cold to care if he caused damage in his haste. It was dusk when he trundled his barrow into the yard. There was no candle flickering behind the curtain. Jim must still be asleep. He'd hoped he'd have the kettle on.

'Come on, Buster, let's get out of the wind. I've got hot pasties and fresh bread and cheese for supper. And I got something tasty for you as well.'

Jim would have bolted the door, so he raised his fist to knock loudly. To his surprise it was open. The room was icy, the fire out, and there was no sign of his friend. The dog trotted into the room showing no sign of disquiet. Alfie's stomach returned to its normal place and he unclenched his fists. For an awful moment he'd thought Ginger or Silas had finally discovered them and Jim had been abducted. If this were the case the dog would be bristling and growling, would have known at once that someone strange had been in the room.

'Where the hell has he gone, Buster? I think he ain't been here for a while, else the fire would be burning.'

He shivered. The first thing to do was get it going again. Wherever Jim was, he'd not want to come back to a freezing room, not when he were feeling so poorly. Eventually it was rekindled and the room warm enough to take off his overcoat. He pulled the kettle over the flames; it wouldn't hurt to have a cup of tea, thaw out a bit, whilst he thought about what to do next.

The window rattled and a gust of icy air swirled around his feet. Where on earth was Jim? What had possessed him to go out when the weather was so bitter? Only then did he see his friend's overcoat hanging where he'd left it the night before. He scrabbled under Jim's bed and pulled out his boots. His friend only had the one pair. He must have gone barefoot. It didn't bear thinking of, being without footwear tonight.

The kettle hissed and he pushed it off the heat. He couldn't settle until he'd found him. He'd nip upstairs and enquire off Mrs Hunter – his land-lady – and George. Maybe they'd seen something. She had the right-hand side of the house and her kitchen window overlooked the backyard; her front parlour faced the street. 'You stop here, Buster. Take care of things. I'm just going upstairs to see if anyone knows where Jim's gone.'

The dog thumped his tail and flopped down in front of the fire, not bothered about going outside again in the cold and dark. He could hear voices in the rooms. Good, someone was in. He knocked on the door and waited.

'Alfie, what can we do for you?' The daughter, Elsie, smiled up at him, her ruined teeth spoiling her appearance.

'I was wondering, miss, if you'd seen Jim. I left him behind today – he was not too well – but when I returned just now the room was empty. He's gone out without his boots or his coat on. I was hoping you might have seen him leave, what direction he went, if there was anyone with him?'

The young woman turned and called to her mother. 'Ma, did you see Alfie's friend go out earlier?'

'No, I've only been in meself a little while. I thought he weren't well and was stopping behind today.'

Alfie stepped forward in order to speak directly to Mrs Hunter. 'I left him with a high fever, but he's gone outside with no boots and no coat. The room was icy, the fire out. I reckon he's been gone all day.'

She shook her head, her expression sad. 'You'll not find him in the dark, Alfie. Let's pray a kind soul took him in. He'll not survive without shelter, it's that bitter. I don't envy no one on the streets tonight.'

'That's what I thought. I'm hoping someone from one of the poor-houses might have took him in. I ain't going down there now; I'll visit tomorrow. I'm going to have a look round the area with the dog. If Jim's still in the neighbourhood Buster will sniff him out soon enough.'

He spent a fruitless two hours peering in shop doorways, calling down dark alleys, but to no avail. 'I don't reckon he's round here no more. He's wandered off right and proper. Let's get back, no point in freezing to death.'

In spite of his worry he ate heartily. Buster gobbled down the stale bread and cheese rind then settled in a corner to gnaw his bone. Alfie put the second pie and the iced buns on the shelf alongside the cough mixture he'd bought. He hoped Jim would be back to take some. Each time there were footsteps in the yard he got up, but it were just other residents using the privy.

He slept little, tossing and turning restlessly. In the year they'd been together he'd become accustomed to Jim's snuffling and snoring; the room seemed quiet without him.

Next morning he was up before dawn. He poked the embers into life and threw on a few lumps of coal. He'd get something down him and set off at first light. The back door was frozen solid. He reckoned he'd woken half the house by the time he'd prised it open. A pale sun shone down from a cloudless sky, and everything was thick with frost. Even the privy sparkled; pity the smell didn't match its appearance. Mind you, it were a lot better when the contents were frozen solid.

His breath steamed in front of him; his feet crunched on the ice. It looked pretty, but he pitied the poor buggers who'd not found a bed last night. He was determined to find his friend today, even if it meant knocking on every door until someone told him something. Going so close to the dosshouse, even after so long, meant there was a risk he might be recognised. His enemies would be on him before he could return to the safety of his own place. Taking his dog with him would keep him safe from attack, but the animal was a dead giveaway. If anyone *was* still looking, it would be for a youth and a big brown dog. The animal was better guarding the money.

'I'll not be gone long, old fellow. I'm going to find our Jim and bring him home. Don't you let anyone in, you understand?'

The dog cocked an ear and lazily opened one eye, then settled back to snooze. He'd been out in the yard to cock his leg and do his business. Alfie had scooped the mess up and tossed it in the privy. There were old ladies who collected dog shit, sold it to the tanneries or something. It was free and plentiful on the streets of London, but it weren't something he'd like to do.

In his thick coat, muffler wrapped around his face, his cap pulled down over his ears, he was unrecognisable as the boy who'd lived in Half

Moon Street. He was a man now. He took the route along Norton Folgate, which led into Bishopsgate Street, mingling with the crowd. No one would pick him out as anyone particular. He'd try the London Workhouse first and then go to Bishopsgate after.

He crossed the road; strolling on the side furthest from his old haunt gave him added protection. The pathways were busy – it was business as usual around here. Folks had to get to work, housewives had to shop, never mind the weather. Still, the city looked pretty enough, soot-streaked buildings silver-coated like something out of one of them picture books Ma had read to Tommy.

He blinked; losing Jim so unexpectedly reminded him of his little brother's death. He kept his eyes skinned for his friend. His heart stopped when he saw a huddle of old clothing in a shop doorway. He bent down to look more closely. It was an old man, stiff as a board. He'd obviously been dead some time, but no one took no notice.

A bit further on he saw two children, clinging together like sparrows in a nest, their scrawny bodies clothed in rags, their lips and feet blue with cold. He dipped into his pocket and handed them a shilling each. They were too cold to speak, but the gratitude in their eyes was enough to make him feel a bit better about finding Jim. If he could help children in distress, then maybe someone had done the same for his mate.

Jim wasn't a child, but then he weren't an adult grown neither. He reckoned his friend was about his age, fifteen, but he looked younger because of his size. Mind you, Alfie looked several years older, already a head taller than most women and eye to eye with a lot of men. His shoulders were broad, his arms well-muscled from the year he'd spent shovelling coal. Sarah wouldn't recognise him, but then maybe he'd not know her either.

He screwed his face up trying to fathom how old she was. She must be seventeen this year. For a girl that was fully grown. She could be courting. Ma had been married not much older than that. Would he ever see her again? He squared his shoulders and raised his head. His business were doing well, he'd got decent savings hidden away, and in a month or two he could start looking about for his own premises. Maybe he would take the train to Colchester one fine day. .

He was so lost in thought he was at his destination before he knew it. Half Moon Street was opposite and the turning to the workhouse the next one. He must risk his neck and cross the road busy with diligences, carts and hackney carriages. He waited for a decent gap in the traffic and, after dodging through, arrived safely on the other side. His boots were liberally smeared with manure. He'd better get rid of that before he knocked at the workhouse.

He wasn't sure how he should do this. Did he bang on the door and ask if they'd taken someone in? Did you have to be a relative to enquire after an inmate? He dithered, gazing in despair at the grim building. Its high wall made it look like a prison, the heavy wooden gates adding to this impression. The inmates were kept as secure as prisoners – that's for sure. He saw the tall hat of a constable approaching and without a second thought Alfie stopped him.

'Excuse me, sir, me friend wandered off yesterday from Hog Lane whilst I was out working. He was right poorly, had a fever and went off without his boots and coat. I've searched everywhere but I ain't found him. I was wondering if he might have been taken in there. Where do I go to enquire?'

The man pulled his whiskers. 'If you go to the side door, you'll see it plain enough. Just ring the bell and someone will come. You can ask them. Let's hope you find your friend safe, young man. It wasn't a night to be out, especially if you ain't got your boots on.'

'Thank you, sir, I'll do that. I see the gate now.'

The peeler tipped his hat and strode off. Alfie approached the gate, not sure if he wanted to know if Jim *was* in there. He had a bad feeling about this; the constable had shaken his head like his landlady. They didn't hold out much hope. The London Workhouse was a bleedin' long way from Hog Lane. Was it likely Jim could have ended up here?

He rapped on the door, his knuckles making little sound. Then he spotted a metal rod hanging from the archway. He grasped the knob, wincing as the metal burned his hand. A hideous clanging echoed behind the wall. He was about to ring again when a flap in the door was wrenched open. A pasty-faced woman glared out at him, her eyes like currants in a bun, her greasy grey hair stuffed under a filthy cap.

'What you want?'

'I was wondering if you'd taken anyone in last night. This is the only place I can think my friend could have ended up.'

'Wait here, I'll make enquiries.'

The opening slammed shut. He danced from foot to foot in an effort to keep warm. It was an age before the mean face stared at him again.

'No one came in last night. I should try the hospital – he's more like to have been taken there.'

Alfie wanted to ask where the hospital was, but considering her duty done the slattern crashed the hatch shut. He'd have to try to Bishopsgate Workhouse next. He'd cut back down Bishopsgate and turn left into Dunnings Lane. This time he knew the drill and located the door he needed without assistance. No one had seen Jim there either.

His last hope was gone. What he needed was to find another peeler; they seemed to know what's what. He didn't think Jim could have ended up in the London Hospital. He'd not have staggered that far the condition he'd been in yesterday. He shivered, remembering something he'd heard when he was working on the coal lighter. Someone had said the boy who'd worked for Black Ben previously had been so badly beaten he'd had to go to the hospital but died within its walls. No one came out of those sorts of places alive.

No, he was missing something here. Jim must have been taken in by someone nearby. He'd get back directly and start banging on doors. He'd come on a wild goose chase; should have been going in the opposite direction, to the shops as well, making enquiries there. He retraced his steps, stopping off briefly at his lodgings to collect Buster. Maybe the dog would sniff his friend out for him. He'd had no luck last night, but it was a bit warmer now and that might help.

He spent the rest of the day asking. Folks shook their heads sadly; no one had seen Jim and no one had much hope of him having survived the cold. Alfie was mystified – ill and dressed as he was, how could Jim have left the neighbourhood?

The store was quiet. Most folk would be at work or at home eating their midday meal. It would do no harm to enquire in here – he'd asked everywhere else already. The proprietor, Mr Beamish, whose name belied his nature, was busy emptying the last grains of rice from a sack into a tin on the counter.

'Not come back then, Alfie?'

'You know I'm looking for my Jim? He's been gone two days now and not a sign of him anywhere.'

'The whole street knows he's gone. Word spreads fast. You're both well thought of round here. You know what's a mystery to me? Why no one has seen him. Mind, as he wandered off in the dark, sensible folks would have been inside keeping warm.'

'But he didn't, mister, he left in broad daylight, when I were out working. I can't understand why no one saw him at all. There was folks around on the streets, there always is, and walking as he was without his coat and boots he'd have stuck out round here. Not many folks without no footwear in this part of the city.'

'True enough. I've been asking customers this morning, but nothing doing so far. They'll spread the word. Someone must know where he is. You'll find him eventually – don't fret.' The shopkeeper swept up the few spilt grains and polished the counter with his shirtsleeve. 'Have you tried at the rectory? The rector's wife and daughter do good works and they might have taken him in out of charity.'

Alfie thought this unlikely. He'd seen these two, a hatchet-faced woman and her daughter no better. They rarely walked around here; the folk were too common for the likes of them. They travelled in style and always had a maidservant with them. Hardly the sort of women who'd take someone off the street, more likely to drive on past. He'd go and ask, but good Samaritans were in short supply there in his opinion.

'Ta, Mr Beamish, I'll nip along right away. Whilst I'm here, any deliveries need doing?'

'Not today. Come in again on Friday – might have something for you then.'

The visit to the rectory proved another wasted journey. He got no further than a maidservant at the back door who sent him packing double quick. He was told in no uncertain terms that the master weren't in the habit of taking people off the streets. There was a perfectly good workhouse for *that* sort of person. God-fearing they might be, but full of Christian charity, they certainly wasn't.

It was too late to go out now and tomorrow he must go back to work. He'd have to hope that word was sent round to him about Jim's whereabouts. There was a hospital, but it was at least forty-five minutes' walk from here, not worth checking to see if his friend had managed to stagger that far. It were more likely he'd collapsed nearby – he'd been too sick to get any further.

Alfie prepared to spend a second night without his friend for company. He reviewed what had happened. What was he missing? Was it possible Buster didn't react because it had been one of the gang who'd taken Jim away? Wouldn't they have stopped to give him his coat and let him put on his boots? It didn't make sense no matter from which way he looked at it. People didn't just vanish into thin air, did they?

He flopped back on his bed too dispirited to hook the curtain across the window or eat the last remaining pasty. He gave the one that had been meant for Jim to Buster for his supper. The temperature dropped. His windows were as icy inside as they were out. He couldn't afford to waste heat by not pulling the curtain across. Using extra coal didn't make sense, especially now he was the only one bringing in money. A freezing draught came under his door as someone braved the elements to use the privy before turning in.

George had offered to help to look on Sunday when he had his day off. With luck Jim would have been found before then. Tomorrow there was a market where the middling folks purchased goods. He'd tried the Saturday night market where the poorest bought the makings for Sunday dinner, the womenfolk waiting outside the beerhouses to get their housekeeping after their men had been paid. These, although busier than the one he was going to next day, were frequented by those what carried their own goods. Their money was so scarce they hadn't even a copper to spare for him to take their laden baskets home on his barrow.

He couldn't afford to sit moping about. He'd done all he could; he must get on with his life or he'd go under. There were a few regular customers who looked out for him, knew he was honest and wouldn't filch their goods on the way back. There were no grand establishments in this vicinity but there were a fair few well-to-do with substantial properties. It was them what were happy to have him deliver stuff. He'd have to find another boy to help with the big barrow at the next furniture sale. Too soon to think of replacing someone he'd begun to think of as a brother and not just a business partner.

He kept busy until dusk, had no time to think about his loss. The room that had once seemed like home now seemed cheerless and empty. Even Buster failed to make it a happy place. His enquiries had uncovered no further news of Jim. All that was left of him was his overcoat and boots, and his share of the money they had put by. He began to think he might have imagined he'd ever had a business partner.

George Benson rapped on his door that evening. 'Alfie, I'd like to borrow a barrow again tomorrow, first thing, if that's all right? I've a nice bit of timber put by and the gaffer needs me to clear it out or some other bugger's going to get it instead. We could keep an eye out for Jim on the way.'

'You're welcome. I ain't got much on, and without Jim I only need a small one. You need a hand? I'll be glad to come along and help.'

'I reckon the big one would be better, because I could do it with one journey. I works in a yard about half an hour from here. If I get there early the master says I can take it then. As long as I'm back at starting time he'll not dock me wages.'

'Suits me – I can tout for work after.'

* * *

It took the two of them to push the laden barrow back over the cobbled streets. It was piled high with off-cuts, broken planks and bits fit only for burning. When they arrived Alfie was gasping, had to support himself on the handle. When he recovered his breath sufficiently to speak he straightened, mopped his face on his sleeve, and turned to his new friend.

'I reckon there's enough to make a couple of tables and a bench and maybe a bookshelf as well. Shall I get started planing the wood for you? I don't have the heart to go to the market at the moment.'

'There's two ladies down Worship Street after bookshelves – make a start on that. It's bloody cold to work outside, but I suppose you're used to it by now.'

'I'll light the brazier, use the off-cuts. I'll be warm enough. I think I'm best cut out for carpentry. Jim says he'll run the delivery side of things and I can concentrate on making furniture with you. I reckon we could start looking for premises as soon as Jim's back.'

George nodded. 'You learnt more in the past year than I did in three. I'll start looking for somewhere suitable right away.'

* * *

London, February 1844

As the days passed Alfie had almost resigned himself to never seeing Jim again. He folded his friend's coat carefully and put it on his empty bed along with his boots. He wouldn't get rid of any of it, nor consider the money his, not until he was sure his mate had gone for good. It was as if Jim had never existed; the small space he'd made in the world had closed up.

He was scraping the last of his vegetable stew from his bowl when Buster raised his head, his lips curled, and a deep, threatening growl filled the room. There was a knock on the door. It was a person his dog didn't know.

8

Alfie hesitated, taking his dog's adverse reaction to indicate it was someone who wished him ill outside the door. The knock was repeated.

'Open the door, if you please. I have urgent news for you.'

This was no villain, not the usual type any road. With Buster at his side ready to spring to his defence if necessary, he'd risk it. He stood behind the door, his heart pounding, his mouth dry. 'Who is it? Name yerself.'

'Mr Hudson. I've come about your friend Jim.'

Alfie flung the door open. Facing him was a sombre gentleman in a many-caped overcoat, his hat pulled down low over his ears and a woolly muffler around his face. Toffs didn't look like this. Had he made a dreadful mistake?

Buster stopped growling and his tail thumped the wall. He trusted his dog's instinct and relaxed, stepping aside to let the man in.

'I'm Alfie Nightingale, Mr Hudson. I've been that desperate for news about Jim but given up hope of ever hearing.'

'I am the benefactor and trustee of a charity that takes care of street children. Your friend Jim was picked up by one of the wardens.'

'Why would he leave his warm bed, mister, when he was so poorly? I can't understand how he ended up in the street; he could scarcely move when I left for work that morning.'

'It was his delirium, young man. It would appear that he set out looking for someone called Ginger. He reached Worship Street and collapsed. If Jarvis had not been driving past at that precise moment he would surely have perished where he fell.'

Jim found, and snug and warm in some mission? Alfie could hardly believe it, could feel his spirits lifting, his face cracking in a smile. 'If you care to take a seat, sir, I'll get me coat and such, and collect Jim's things; he'll need them to come home.'

The gentleman had removed his hat and loosened the scarf around his face. He cleared his throat. 'I should leave those here, my boy. They'll likely go missing if you take them at the moment. Fetch them later, when Jim's able to accompany you.'

'How did you find me? Did Jim give you my direction?'

'No, a constable brought in two children he'd found freezing to death in a shop doorway in Bishopsgate Street. When he called back to enquire after their welfare we mentioned having found your friend. He recalled speaking to you outside the London Workhouse a while ago. After that it was a simple matter of asking a shopkeeper for information. It seems that everyone knew you were searching for your friend.'

'I was that. I can't tell you how happy I am to see you, mister. I'm ready to go. No, Buster, you stop here. They'll not allow dogs where I'm going. I'll be back later with news of our Jim.'

In the icy passage he hesitated a moment, not sure if he should lock his door or leave it as it was. If there was a fire no one could release his dog, but if the door somehow came open Buster might well come out to look for him. He couldn't risk their secret hoard being taken.

He locked the door. Mr Hudson had already vanished into the yard, retrieving a lantern he'd left burning just outside. It were odd the gentleman coming to the back gate, not knocking on the front door, but not to worry. All that mattered was he was going to see Jim, and when he was well bring him home again. They went down the narrow side passage and waiting outside was a hackney carriage.

'Crikey! I ain't never been in one of those. We're to travel in style then, sir?'

'We are indeed, young man. It is too far for us to walk.' He smiled, his teeth flashing white under the flickering gas lamp. 'At least it is too far me – I'm not as young as I used to be, as no doubt you have observed.'

The gentleman was past middle age, but not elderly by any means. When he'd removed his hat, his hair had been grey all right, but thick, and it matched his handsome side whiskers. He was otherwise clean-shaven, and smartly, if sombrely dressed. His trousers, what could be seen of them, were of a dark material, his boots black and well made.

Alfie scrambled into the hackney carriage, clutching the strap as it rocked. Briefly the interior was illuminated and he looked around with interest. There was a scuffed leather seat, more than room enough for two, but it smelt of stale tobacco and sweat. He reckoned he'd rather be walking in the fresh air than cooped up inside one of these vehicles.

This cove must be wealthy – it weren't cheap to travel in a hackney cab. He'd said he was the benefactor or some such of this charitable home; he was obviously not short of a few bob. Jim had been lucky; this mission place sounded a sight better than a workhouse.

'Does we owe you anything, mister? As you can see, we ain't badly off. Jim and me – he's my business partner – we own three barrows and do a decent trade. We reckon to rent our own premises next year if we continue busy like what we are now.'

'You are a hard-working young man. I was aware of that the moment I saw you. And a good and loyal friend to Jim.' He cleared his throat again, and Alfie heard him shifting in the darkness. 'I must warn you, Alfie, Jim is not at all well. However, we must not dwell on that now. He will be much restored to have you come to visit. He's been asking after you constantly these past days.' He cleared his throat for a third time; it was beginning to annoy Alfie. 'I can assure you, we require no recompense from you. It is a charity and most of the people we assist are completely without funds.'

He stopped talking as the vehicle swayed and bounced around the corner before straightening, the jarvey cracking his whip and urging his nag into something resembling a trot.

'It was because Jim came out without his boots and coat we thought he was destitute. But as soon as he was able he quite forcibly disabused us of this fact. But as our mission is in Wood Street, and he had no recollection of where he was, he found it difficult to tell us exactly how to find you.'

Alfie cursed his decision not to tell Jim the name of the street they lived on. He'd thought that if Jim was ever waylaid by Silas Field, or Ginger and the gang, he'd be unable to give away the whereabouts of their lodgings. If Jim had known he lived on Hog Lane he would have been returned to him days ago, not have been left among strangers all this time.

It was a full thirty minutes before the vehicle shuddered to a halt. They were outside an imposing building with stone steps and a portico. It looked too grand to house foundlings. Mr Hudson waited until the jarvey dropped down from his perch to open the door. Coins exchanged hands and then the cab moved off.

He was to make his own way back then. Bugger that! He could read the street signs, but he had no idea where Wood Lane was; he'd never find his way in the dark. He'd face that problem when he came to leave. He didn't want to go anywhere without Jim, but he weren't well enough to leave – that was obvious. He frowned. What about Buster? He couldn't abandon his dog for more than a few hours. He'd have to return at first light whatever happened.

He shrugged, running after Mr Hudson as he ascended the front steps. Why not go around the back? He'd not be admitted roughly dressed as he was. The gentleman rapped sharply on the door. It was opened by a uniformed servant. She curtsied and they were ushered in. This weren't like any hospital he'd ever heard of. It was set up like the residence of some toff. He hovered uncertainly behind Mr Hudson, glancing sideways at the family portraits hanging on the wall, the clean carpet that ran down the centre of the wide hallway. Then he got a whiff of something he recognised, carbolic soap, and then boiled cabbage and unwashed boys.

The gentleman handed his outer garments to the maid; she waited patiently whilst he did the same. He weren't so sure about this. He hoped he saw them again, that they didn't disappear forever. He felt out of place.

Someone like him should have been taken in the back like other common folk.

Mr Hudson saw his disquiet. 'No doubt you are surprised by this building. The front rooms are occupied by the warden and his wife and, when I'm in town, I stay here also. The house servants reside in the attics. However, as you will see, the rear of the house has been substantially extended to accommodate dormitories, wards and recreation spaces for our children.'

He sniffed and his eyes crinkled at the corners. 'Although we keep separate, you are always aware of the real purpose of this place. Come along, Alfie, you must be desperate to see your friend after having given up so much of your valuable time searching for him.'

He led the way along the corridor and down a short flight of stairs. Facing them was a substantial door. He knocked, and hurrying feet arrived behind it. There was the sound of a bolt being undone, a key turned and the door swung back.

This time it was no uniformed maid, but a skinny woman in a starched cap, long white apron and shiny gown. She curtsied. 'Good evening, sir, we've been expecting you. I take it this is the young man Jim has been asking for?'

Mr Hudson nodded. 'Indeed it is, Mrs Jones. May I introduce you to Alfie Nightingale.'

The woman smiled, and Alfie saw her stiff appearance was misleading. She had kind eyes and her smile was sympathetic. 'I'm so pleased to see you. Come along with me. Your friend is in a side room.'

The corridor looked and smelled like an institution. This was obviously a hospital wing, but noisy feet and the sound of laughter came from somewhere further away. If there was laughter in here, it weren't such a bad place; no one laughed in a workhouse. The nurse stopped outside the door. It was slightly ajar, but he could hear no sounds from within it. Jim must be asleep. It was after nine o'clock, but he'd soon wake up to speak to him.

He stepped into a small room, just large enough for a large metal bed, a chair and washstand. A decent fire burned in the grate, an oil lamp stood on a side table, but this must be the wrong place. That couldn't be Jim resting so still in the centre of the white sheets.

He clutched the door frame. They hadn't told him his friend was at death's door. No wonder Mr Hudson had been so keen to get him here that he'd been prepared to pay for a hackney cab. He rushed forward, dropping onto the edge of the bed, the only sound in the room the rasp of Jim's laboured breathing. The heat from his body burned through the thin coverings.

'Jim, Jim, it's me. It's Alfie come to see you.' There was no response. He clasped his friend's skeletal hand and tried again. 'Jim, wake up. I ain't going to sit here talking to meself all night.' The blue eyelids flickered and opened.

'Alfie, I'm right glad to see you. You took your time. Almost missed me, you did.' The words were little more than a hoarse whisper and the effort tired him. His eyes shut and the hideous sound of his breathing continued.

He gently squeezed Jim's hand. It was little more than a week since he'd seen him; how could he have lost so much weight that his shape barely made a dent under the sheets? 'Don't you fret, Jim, I'll see you through this. We've got plans, you and me; you're me business partner. I want you back beside me fighting fit.'

The faintest flicker of a smile crossed Jim's face. 'Promise me, you ain't going to leave me on me own? I'm scared. I need you with me.' His voice was a thin thread in the silence. Alfie's eyes brimmed over.

'I ain't going nowhere, Jim. You're as good as a brother to me. You're the best mate I've ever had. I'm not leaving without you – you have my word on that.'

'Remember, Alfie, everything I got I leave to you and Buster. You get that yard, keep me name on the barrows so you'll not forget me.'

There was a brief pressure on Alfie's hand, then Jim – exhausted by the effort – went quiet again. The nurse and Mr Hudson had left him alone. He was glad of that. He and Jim didn't need anyone else; they were a team, weren't they?

He sniffed, but his nose continued to run. His cheeks were wet, but he wasn't going to let go of Jim's hand to rummage for the rag. 'Don't give up,

Jim. Don't you dare die on me. You're me best mate. We're going to make a fortune, find ourselves two pretty girls one day and get married. I can't do it on me own; it won't be the same if you ain't here.'

The grip on his hand tightened briefly, and then with a final shuddering breath the room was silent. Alfie waited, willing his friend's chest to rise, for him to take another gasp, but nothing happened. Instead, the hand in his went slack. Just like that – his life was snuffed out.

He collapsed across the body, his grief far worse than it had been when Tommy had drowned. He sobbed, inconsolable. His dreams had ended with the death of his friend.

Then he felt movement behind him and gentle arms reached round to remove him from the bed. 'Come along, Alfie, Jim's gone to a better place now. Thank the good Lord that you got here in time. He was hanging on until he could speak to you.' Mrs Jones drew him away from the corpse that had once been his friend. 'When he was able, he talked of nothing else but how you'd rescued him. You made him very happy.'

Alfie choked and wiped his nose and eyes on his sleeve. He didn't care what they thought of his manners – his best friend in the world was dead. He couldn't imagine carrying on the business on his own.

'I am taking you down to the kitchen. Cook will take care of you, and when you're recovered Mr Hudson wishes to speak to you.'

He slumped into a chair and a hot mug was placed in his grip. He tried to lift it, but the contents slopped onto the table.

'Let me do it for you, Alfie. Here, swallow this down; it'll make you feel much better.'

It was lifted to his mouth and he drank. The hot tea warmed him, the sweetness a pleasant surprise. Jim had given everything he owned to him. He didn't need it; he wanted nothing without his friend to share it. He'd use the money to give Jim a good send-off – that's what he'd do.

He finished his drink, replacing the mug carefully on the table. The cook nodded and refilled it from an enormous brown china teapot. 'Have another one, and then I'll get you something to eat. Shock can do funny things to a body.'

'Thank you, madam. I'm feeling more meself now.' His voice sounded strange, as if it was someone else speaking. He was in a large kitchen sitting at a scrubbed pine table. All around him were gleaming pots and pans. A massive kitchen range filled one end of the room. It was similar to the one Ma had used back in Colchester but many times bigger.

Sitting opposite him was Mr Hudson, not fussing nor prosing on about heaven, just waiting quietly until he'd finished his tea and was ready to listen. There was another cove beside him, in waistcoat and shirt-sleeves; they were both drinking tea from the same sort of mug he was using.

'Mr Hudson, it's all my fault. If I'd taken Jim to the hospital, not gone to work that day, he wouldn't have died.'

'It wasn't your fault, Alfie. The physician said he had congestion of the lungs. It was so far advanced when we found him he would have died wherever he'd been. Do not blame yourself. He was weakened from his years of living on the street. Console yourself with the thought that his last years on this earth were the happiest he'd experienced.'

The other man nodded solemnly. 'It was his time. We cannot question God's will. He is in a place without pain or suffering. Rejoice in that, my boy.'

Alfie didn't want to hear this hogwash about a better place, a wise and a benevolent God. If that were true, why did he let children die of starvation in the streets whilst others lived like kings?

'I have enough to pay for the funeral. I've got to get off home now; I'll come back tomorrow with the money.'

Mr Hudson shook his head. 'That will not be necessary, Alfie. Jim wouldn't want you spending any of his precious savings on that. The foundation is here to help. It's what we do. No one gives up their life under this roof and gets a pauper's burial. They are all buried decently, and given a small headstone to mark the grave. Tell me, what would you like written on his?'

For a second time Alfie was overwhelmed by his loss. He stared at the table, swallowing the lump in his throat and willing his tears back. 'Put, "*Here lies Jim, the best friend anyone could have. Rest in peace.*" That'll do, thanks, mister.'

He glared, daring them to contradict him. The man in the waistcoat smiled. 'Very fitting. Your words shall be exactly what is carved on the headstone. You will be able to visit the grave and see for yourself later on. Do you wish to spend the night here or return to your lodgings?'

Having something practical to think about helped him gain control of his emotions. 'I have to be back at first light. Me dog's shut in the room and won't take kindly to being left.'

The men exchanged glances. 'That's what we thought. Mr Hudson dismissed the hackney carriage. It doesn't do to keep a beast standing about in this weather. However, we shall summon another to return you to your lodgings.'

Alfie interrupted him. 'I'm happy to walk back. You've done more than enough for us already. Give us the directions – I'll get back all right. And I'll find me away back for the funeral too. Just tell me when it will be.'

Mr Hudson pulled his whiskers. 'You're a fine young man, Alfie Nightingale. Your attitude does you credit. Do you read, by any chance?' Alfie nodded, for the first time truly proud of his accomplishment. 'Excellent, I shall write the directions down for you. I don't suppose you've eaten tonight so I insist that you eat some supper before you leave. Are you quite certain you wish to walk back? It will take you an hour or more and it's already past ten o'clock.'

'I spend all me time outside, in all weathers, sir. I ain't familiar with the streets round here, but I'll soon learn them.'

'Your friend's funeral will be tomorrow; it is best these things are done immediately. Can you be back here at noon? We have our own chapel. The service shall be conducted there, then the hearse will transport the coffin to the cemetery.'

The mention of a coffin caused Alfie to shudder. He stared at the table, gripping his chair to steady himself. A large plate of beef stew, dumplings floating on the surface, was plonked in front of him. He thought he wouldn't be able to eat, that his grief had stolen his appetite, but the savoury smell wafting up from the plate made his mouth water. He'd not eaten anything so tasty since he'd left Colchester. Maybe this was a sign from the Almighty that it was time he returned and found his family.

9

LONDON, MARCH 1844

Alfie felt numb. He survived by filling every minute of the day with work. He trundled his barrow from place to place, market to market – dropping his rates when he didn't get immediate work. He returned to his lonely room each night too exhausted to mourn; even Buster began to look thin and dejected. When he wasn't delivering he was making tables and benches for George.

The weather deteriorated. Although the snow made things more difficult for pedestrians and carriages alike, more folks were eager to have their groceries and such delivered. Carrying large baskets of vegetables, household provisions and other paraphernalia become an exercise fraught with danger. The cobbles and pathways were permanently icy; one slip could mean a broken limb and no work. Then it would be the workhouse for everyone in the family.

The only glimmer of hope, the one thing that kept him sane, was his friendship with the man upstairs. George Benson got him to shift stuff regularly; sometimes it was completed pieces of furniture from the yard he worked at, but more often it was a load of off-cuts. Of a Sunday they worked together building bookshelves, tables, and the occasional cradle.

They were obliged to do this in the backyard of the lodging house. Mrs Hunter wouldn't hear of them working indoors. Buster refused to remain outside when they were hammering and banging; he snoozed by the fire, content as long as he could hear his master close by. Alfie noticed his dog had become more possessive, quicker to snarl at a stranger, since Jim had died. It was as if the dog was worried his special person might disappear one day like Jim had done.

George told him he was a competent carpenter now, had learnt better than most apprentices did in five years. Alfie took pleasure in making something solid. But often the tools, even with their wooden handles, became ice-coated and too slippery to use safely.

One day, on impulse, he walked the hour and a half to the cemetery to leave a bedraggled bunch of violets on the mound of earth. Jim's grave was still marked by a simple wooden cross with a number painted on it. The headstone wouldn't be positioned until the ground settled.

By the middle of March he'd begun to rent out the spare handcarts; he wouldn't make as much renting out, but he had no need for more than one. He charged two shillings a week for the smaller, three shillings and sixpence for the big one. He would still be adding to his savings. When he'd got a pony saved, he'd pack his bags and go back to Colchester.

He'd had enough of city life, the dirt and grime, the constantly looking over his shoulder in case one of the gang, or one of Silas Field's bully boys, was creeping up behind him. More often than not Buster opted to remain at home. The snow split and cracked his pads, the ice freezing between his toes. His beloved companion might well be feeling his years. If anything happened to the dog that would be it. He wouldn't want to live without him at his side; it would be unthinkable.

He spoke to George about his plans one Sunday. Compared to the bitter months that had gone it was pleasant outside in the yard. Buster had deigned to join them today, was gnawing on a large bone one of the neighbours had chucked him. The dog was well liked by everyone in the terrace. They reckoned there'd been no pilfering of coal from the yard since he'd moved in. They were putting the finishing touches to a dresser ordered by the newly married couple in a cottage over the back.

'George, I'm going to back to Colchester in a few weeks. I'll need to sell the barrows. Are you interested?'

'I am. With all the extra I've been making since we've been working together I've got more than enough to pay three months up front on a decent yard. I found one that has a cottage goes with it. The place is near derelict and will need a deal of work before I can move in.'

'Good for you! I'm happy to give you a hand doing it up, but I'm off the end of April – come what may.'

George put down his rag. 'Why don't you still come in with me? You could organise the deliveries, employ a couple of boys to work for you. You can work alongside. You'll be a real asset to me, and we could take on bigger jobs together.'

'That's kind of you to offer, but no. I want to get back. I've been away too long already. I have a sister in Colchester. We was always close, and I need to know how she fares. I thought I'd set myself up as a carpenter. I reckon I can make tables and such as good as you nowadays.'

'Fair enough, but I'll miss you, Alfie. You're a mate. If you stick to what I've learnt you – don't go for anything fancy, mind – you'll do well enough.'

They continued to polish the dresser. George was a good bloke to work with, didn't natter on all day, left you to your own thoughts unless he had something useful to say. It was getting chilly by the time they'd finished.

'There, let's get this on the big barrow and deliver it before it gets dark.' George waited whilst Alfie removed the two smaller carts and wheeled the large one over. When they were trundling down Hog Lane, Alfie paused to check the rope was secure.

'Jim and I had intended to go to the opening of that new tunnel what goes under the river.'

'The Thames Tunnel? I'd like to see that. When's it open then?'

'On the 25th March. You can buy a penny ticket and go right inside. It will be my final farewell to Jim. His headstone's going up in a couple of weeks. After that I reckon I can think about leaving.'

'We'll go together, make a day of it, have supper out and a pint or two to celebrate. I'll give in me notice and finish the day before. Will you help me do up me cottage before you go? I only need two of your barrows really, but I'll take all three. I can rent them out like what you do. You'll give me a good deal, as I'm your mate, won't you, Alfie?'

He slapped his friend on the back. 'You can pay what I did, and they were in a shoddy state then, not painted and running smooth like what they do now.' He rubbed his back. Pushing a laden cart over the cobbles weren't easy. 'I'll help until I leave. Will that do you?'

He told his landlady he was leaving at the end of April. She'd agreed to buy back his furniture when he went, which would give him a few more bob to add to his savings. He would have surpassed his target of £25 by a considerable margin by then.

Each week, when he had five pounds, he'd been exchanging his coins for paper notes. These he intended to stitch into his waistcoat lining – no thieving bugger would find them even if he was done over. He scratched Buster's head. No one would dare do that, not with his dog at his side, but better safe than sorry.

* * *

Spring rushed in. Flowers appeared in patches of bare soil, a haze of green covered the hedges where he walked first thing with his dog. With the end of the hard winter, his optimism returned. He yearned to be back in the countryside; to stroll in open fields, to breathe air that wasn't heavy with soot, to walk on pavements that were clean.

In his mind's eye he saw Colchester as the perfect place – prosperous and well-cared-for. Streets gaslit, with a brand-new hospital, workhouse, and other municipal buildings. He'd rent himself lodgings before he went to look for Sarah. He smiled. No, he'd get himself a little cottage in Maidenburgh Street, behind the castle. If he remembered rightly, there was a row of decent places along there and more often than not there was one or two vacant. It was close to the river meadows as well. He couldn't recall if any of them had a yard big enough to put a handcart.

'You'll like it in the country, Buster. Rabbits to chase, the ground soft under your paws, friendly faces everywhere and our own home to live in. I'll put me money in the bank, set meself up proper and then go round to see Ma.'

He thought maybe he'd stopped growing. He hadn't had to replace his boots this year because his toes was being crushed against the end. His trousers weren't halfway up his ankles; they remained where they should be, resting on his boots. He was only an inch or two shorter than George, and his friend was a fine-looking man.

He ran his fingers across his upper lip and felt the roughness of hair. It wouldn't be long before he had to buy a razor and start shaving. He was a man. He could take care of himself. He couldn't wait to get back home and show Sarah how well he'd done. He'd have so much to tell her, and he could start with the opening of the Thames Tunnel.

* * *

The morning of March the 25th dawned sunny. No cold east wind – it was a perfect spring day. Alfie had bought himself a smart carpetbag ready for his return, plus a new suit of clothes. He was the proud possessor of three cotton shirts, two waistcoats, spare trousers and three pairs of socks. He now had all his vests and underwear laundered regular and took himself off to a bathhouse. He enjoyed immersing himself in hot water, being completely clean and fresh. He bore no resemblance to the half-formed boy who had run away from Black Ben.

'You stop here, Buster. I ain't taking you with me today. You'll not like the crowds, and I don't want to be picked out by anyone. Ginger and the gang will be working and they'd spot you soon enough. You stay in the yard and eat your bone.' His dog had had a long walk that morning and would be happy to snooze the rest of the day away.

There was savings clubs for the likes of him run by the unions, but he weren't going to get involved with any of that political stuff. The Chartists might be right – rich folk had everything and the poor a rotten deal – but marches and protests wasn't his style. He'd leave the toffs to get on with it if they left him to live his life the way he wanted.

He checked the dog's water container was full and the yard gate shut, and he was ready. He ran up the stairs and banged on George's door. It opened immediately.

'Alfie, you look a real gent. If I'd known you was putting on your Sunday best I'd have made more of an effort.'

His friend looked his usual dapper self. His yellow cravat neatly tied, his brown tweed jacket and trousers freshly sponged and his boots good and shiny. 'Fishing for compliments? I reckon we'll turn the heads of a few young ladies today. I don't want to be back too late. I'm off first thing tomorrow to an auction and it's a fair distance away.'

'I'll be glad to get started on the cottage. My governor weren't too happy about me leaving, I can tell you.' He grinned, looking more Alfie's age than a young man of almost twenty. 'It won't be the same here without you and that Buster. I'm going to make the most of the next few weeks. I reckon with your help I'll be well set up by the time you go.'

'It'll make a change slapping a bit of distemper on the walls. Now, let's get off – there'll be thousands with the same idea. It ain't supposed to be open to the public, according to the leaflet, until six o'clock, but I reckon we're right to go this afternoon. We'll probably have to queue, so the sooner we get there the less time we'll have to wait.'

This was the first time Alfie had ventured near the river. Without his dog, and a head taller and dressed smart, he doubted – even if he came face-to-face with Black Ben – that he'd be recognised. He would enjoy the spectacle today. It would be something to tell his grandchildren about. 'I gave Buster a bath yesterday. He weren't too keen, but I ain't taking him back next month covered in soot.'

'Stop talking about leaving. Let's enjoy ourselves today and not think about the future. I've money in me pocket; I'm ready for anything. We'll join in the fun, watch the fireworks, listen to the band and buy a decent meal and a couple of pints of beer before we go home.'

As they approached Wapping, the streets were bustling with like-minded people. There was a festive atmosphere amongst the crowd, children skipping and laughing, men and women exchanging jokes; everyone in their Sunday best determined to enjoy themselves. It was a wonder and no mistake – a tunnel running right under the Thames.

He could hear the sound of a brass band playing in the distance. He checked the pamphlet again. There were two entrances to the tunnel on this side of the river and the same at Rotherhithe.

'It's a shame folks can't go through in a vehicle – that it's pedestrians only what can use it. Fancy taking all these years and spending all that money and not being able to take goods across as was first intended.'

George nodded solemnly. 'I heard there was problems and the only way they'd got to finish it was by putting spiral staircases at each end. Still, I'm going under. Imagine, being able to walk under a river. It's a blooming miracle – that's what it is.'

There were thousands of other folk ready to experience the novelty. The colourful flags decorating the surrounding streets added to the excitement. He heard a lady in front of him telling her children that people were coming on omnibuses, on horseback, in carriages and specially chartered boats.

Penny tickets were being sold, so fast Alfie was glad he'd had the foresight to purchase his the previous day. There were two marquees, he heard someone say, erected in Cow Court where the dignitaries and their guests were to sit through the speeches. He was enjoying the warm spring sunshine, the feeling of excitement in the air, the thought that the world was changing and he wasn't being left behind.

As they were ticket holders they joined the rear of the crowd pressing towards the entrances. It was a little after two o'clock when suddenly the queue forced itself past the waiting inspectors and began to descend into the tunnel, brandishing their tickets to prove they were not there illegally.

He and George had no choice – they were carried along in the press of people until they reached the top of the spiral staircase. They went down willy-nilly, the folks in front and behind making it difficult to stay upright. Alfie pitied the women in their full skirts with all them layers of petticoats. It was hard enough to negotiate for a gent.

The walls were brilliantly whitewashed, sparkling in the gaslights. He marvelled at the spectacle – and to think he'd seen it before it was officially opened. The ceilings were vaulted, and high. He almost expected to hear the sound of the river running overhead. The glittering globes attached to either side of the walls made it light enough to see down the tunnel. Ahead of him, set in small alcoves, were women selling cheap souvenirs and bits and pieces. He had more sense than to waste his hard-earned money.

There must have been a couple of thousand in the tunnel before they were supposed to be there. They milled about admiring what they saw.

He lost sight of his companion in the crowd. He'd find him soon enough when he got out.

By the time it was his turn to ascend on the far side he'd had more than enough of tunnels. He realised he didn't like being underground. Halfway through he'd begun to feel the walls pressing in on him. Perspiration was trickling between his shoulder blades and his hands were clammy, his heart racing.

It was an effort not to fight his way up the stairs, so desperate was he to get back in the fresh air. George was waiting for him. 'I'm mightily impressed. I can't wait to go back later on today, but we'll have to wait until it's officially opened, and that won't be until after six o'clock.'

'I'm going back by London Bridge. You'll not get me down again for love nor money. Done it once – that's enough for me.'

'Fair enough. There's a coffee stall ahead and I could do with a cup. I'll see you there.' His friend strode off and the crowd closed around him. He sniffed. The distinctive aroma of coffee brewing would make it easy to meet up with George again.

There were as many awaiting the treat on this side of the river as on the other. He felt someone bump into him and instinctively grabbed the hand that had tried to dip into his pocket. His hold was strong, no match for the pickpocket who'd hoped to remove his cash. He spun round and found himself face-to-face with Nelson.

His erstwhile friend seemed to have shrunk since he'd last seen him. He was still dressed in the garments he'd been given the day they'd moved from Half Moon Street. These were as dirty as the ones he'd worn before, his hair as full of crawlers. The real change was in his eyes. They were sunk into his head. How could he be in such dire straits? The boys had had enough money to live like lords for a year or two.

'Nelson, it's me, Alfie. Don't you recognise me?' Immediately he stopped whining and protesting his innocence and his face lit up.

'Bugger me! I'd never have spotted it was you. You look like a toff. Done all right for yourselves then, you and Jim?' He glanced over Alfie's shoulder hopefully. 'Where's Jim? Ain't he here?'

Alfie felt the familiar stab of pain. 'He died a while back, congestion of the lungs. What's happened to you and the rest of them? I didn't think to see you here like this. Last time I saw you, you were well set up. What's going on?'

He checked George was out of earshot, then drew Nelson to one side to continue the conversation. He wanted to find out what calamity had occurred to reduce the boy to such a state.

'Sorry to hear that. Jim was a good friend.' Nervously Nelson glanced over his shoulder before crouching down so he wouldn't be visible in the crowd. 'We all work for Silas now. He got Ginger. We told him to wait, not to try and move that stuff, but you know Ginger, he wouldn't listen.' The boy wiped his snotty nose on his hand. 'Ginger took everything one day, all of it, inside his coat, saying he'd be back with the money that night. We never saw him again. Two days later Silas and his boys turned up. They took what was left. We got beaten something cruel, and well, here we are.'

'What happened to Ginger? Did they kill him?'

'They did, slit his throat, murdered him in cold blood. We was forced to move. We live in a worse dosshouse than Ma Bishop's. There's a dozen of us. We manage the best we can, but it ain't like it used to be, I can tell you.'

'Buy yourself something to eat, Nelson. I wish you well. I'm sorry things ended like this.'

Nelson looked down at the half crown in his grimy hand. 'You're a gent. I always said so – not like us. Good luck to you, Alfie.'

He was gone, slipping through the crowd like an eel. Alfie would never see him again. There was nothing he could do for any of them. They'd chosen their path; he'd chosen his. He was sorry that Ginger had been murdered, the boy had taken him in when he'd been desperate. No one deserved to die that way you. Saddened by the meeting, he turned and forced his way through the crowd to the coffee stall. Today had certainly been a final farewell in more ways than one. George was waiting for him, two mugs in his fists.

'Crickey! You look as though you've seen a ghost. Drink this, Alfie – it'll make you feel more the thing.'

After a few swallows he was restored. 'I could do with something to eat. It's hours since we had breakfast. Shall we go and find a place?'

It was after nine when Alfie finally staggered down the stairs to rescue his dog from the backyard. 'Buster, I got you a meat pie to make up for it. Come on, let's get in. I need to get me head down; I've had one too many beers tonight.'

He tottered over and collapsed onto his bed. 'Here, I didn't forget you when I were out. See, what do you think of your smart red collar and lead?' He buckled on the collar. Buster took umbrage and jerked away. He deigned to gobble up the pie but then turned his back and went to sleep.

The next morning when he attempted to attach the lead the dog growled and shook his head. Alfie thought it prudent not to insist. 'It's for the best, old fellow. They won't let you on the train next month unless you're tied up.'

Happy once the hated leash was removed, the dog wagged his tail. The smart red collar looked grand against his freshly scrubbed fur and the animal seemed proud to be wearing it.

'Right, let's make a bit more money to take home with us. Only a few more weeks and we'll be off. I can't wait to see Sarah's face when she meets you.'

10

COLCHESTER, MARCH 1844

Sarah crept down the attic stairs. She was unwilling to disturb the three Cooper boys who slept in the bedroom on the right of the landing, or Dan and Maria Cooper who slept in the larger bedroom on the left.

As always on laundry day she would have to light the fire under the copper in the scullery. Nelly would be here in an hour or so and would expect the water to be hot. It was light enough to see without using candles or the oil lamps. Her first task was to riddle the grate and get the range back to full heat. She traced her fingers lovingly across the embossed writing that ran boldly across the top – *Hewens' Patent Range*. This had cost Mr Cooper the princely sum of five pounds and fifteen shillings according to Joe Cooper. It was a pity his wife didn't appreciate the wonders of the cooker. The money he'd spent on it was the same as Sarah's wages for a year.

She had been alarmed to find this beautiful object dull and encrusted with grease when she'd arrived in December. This cast-iron contraption was her pride and joy; now it was blackleaded every week and the brass attachments polished to a rich shine. She could produce perfect bread, scones, wonderful stews and anything else she had a fancy to make. It even had a tap on the left-hand side from which she could draw hot water. It made bathing a pleasure instead of a chore.

The kitchen was *her* domain; the Coopers sat in the front room of an evening, leaving her to rock happily in a wooden armchair exactly like the one her ma had used. The boys (Joe, the eldest at seven; Davie, a year younger; and the youngest, John, almost four) drifted back and forth, welcome in either room. She couldn't stand here daydreaming – she had tasks to perform before she went up at six o'clock to tap on Mr Cooper's door.

The dough she had left to prove on the back of the range was well risen. It was the work of moments to knock it back and put it in the greased bread tins. By the time she'd finished her early morning chores, the oven would be hot enough and the bread ready to go in. This morning they would have porridge with sugar *and* cream. It had taken her a while to get used to the fact that in this household there was no shortage at the end of the week. Mr Cooper earned excellent money in his position as foreman at Hawkins timber yard.

He gave her the housekeeping money on a Saturday. Anything left over at the end of the week was hers to keep. He was generous to a fault, a kind and loving father and affectionate husband. She valued the time she spent in his company first thing in the morning; the more she got to know him and his wife the happier she was.

The fire under the copper was taking longer to light than usual; if she didn't hurry she'd be late waking up her employer. She poured out his mug of tea, set his bowl of porridge at his place on the long, scrubbed table and added a small jug of cream. The sugar pot was always in the centre. Both her employers liked to have it in their tea.

She checked her appearance in the shiny base of a large copper pan. Her cap was straight, her apron clean and her face free of smudges. Good – she would go up and knock on the door. Mrs Cooper liked to sleep in. The baby was due in three weeks and the midwife insisted she rested as much as possible. The boys came down after their father had left for work. They were all good sleepers, thankfully.

When Mr Cooper appeared she was just removing the first loaf from the oven, the kitchen filled with the aroma of freshly baked bread. Not something they had been accustomed to until she'd joined the family three months ago.

'Good morning, Mr Cooper. Would you like toasted bread or fresh this morning?'

He yawned and smiled at her. 'Toast, and some of that dripping you made yesterday to go with it, Sarah.'

'How's Mrs Cooper this morning? Did she get any sleep?'

'Not much. I shall be glad when this baby arrives. Maria's not been well throughout her time. But these past weeks she's been much better. It was a godsend you turning up at The Prince of Wales when you did.'

Her cheeks coloured at his praise. 'That's what I say about you, sir, every day since I came to live here. I have a decent position and because of your generosity am able to put a few coppers each week into the savings club.'

He said no more, merely nodded and picked up his spoon. Whilst he munched contentedly she made his toast at the open fire in the centre of the range. There was no need for her to pack him up a midday meal. His place of work, just over the bridge, was no more than ten minutes' distance from the house and he always returned to eat with his family. *He* insisted Sarah sat with them; *she* insisted that Sarah called her by her given name and treated her more like a younger sister than an employee.

The weather was harsh, as cold as it had been in December, but the nights were lighter now, and the promise of spring was in the air. When she returned from checking that the fire under the copper was burning he'd gone. It was six thirty, another hour before the boys woke up and Nelly arrived to do the laundry.

She prepared the vegetables for the midday soup and the evening meal. Tonight they would have shepherd's pie, a firm favourite with the boys. All she had to do was mince the leftover lamb and her chores for the day would be done. She glanced at the little brass clock that stood in pride of place in the centre of the dresser. There was still time for her to eat her breakfast at leisure before taking a tray to Mrs Cooper; she could not bring herself to think of her as Maria even after three months of being asked to do so.

The boys needed little help to dress themselves nowadays. Even John wanted to be like his big brothers and do it himself, sometimes with comical results.

'Joe, I've put out your porridge. I'll pour the tea when I come down. Mrs Beeson is busy in the scullery. Don't be going in there and getting in her way – promise me.'

He grinned. With his mop of dark curls and twinkling blue eyes he was the image of his father. 'Promise, Sarah. How's me ma this morning?'

'She had a restless night, Joe, so I doubt she'll be getting up today. She needs to build up her strength for when the baby comes. It could be any time.'

'We'll draw her picture, won't we, boys? We can take it up when we get back from school.'

'John can come too,' the youngest screeched.

'If you're a good boy we can feed the ducks on the way home. What do you say to that?'

The little boy's frown vanished. 'I like duckies, Sarah.'

Joe and Davie attended the infant school most mornings, but they didn't seem to learn much there. No doubt because there were over forty in the class and only one harassed schoolmistress.

The tea was getting cold – she must take it up. She rested the tray on a small side table outside the marital bedroom. She tapped on the door but didn't wait to be invited in. More often than not she had to wake Mrs Cooper up. It didn't seem natural, sleeping so much and still feeling tired all the time.

'Maria, I have your breakfast here; why don't I help you to sit up?'

'I'm not that hungry, Sarah love, put it down and I'll drink the tea. I feel like a beached whale. The sooner this nipper appears the happier I'll be. The midwife says I'm carrying a lot of water. The baby's small and I thank the Lord for that.' She waved Sarah away and slowly edged back until she was propped against the pillows. Her cheeks were flushed and puffy; she didn't look at all well.

'Here you are, drink this. Nothing like a strong cup of tea to brighten you up. I'll leave the bread and butter here. You might fancy it later.' Sarah knew better than to offer anything more substantial. It was a mystery to her how Mrs Cooper was so big when she ate barely enough to keep a fly alive. 'Nelly's here; I'd better get back to the kitchen. John isn't safe around the hot water.'

* * *

The mistress retired early complaining of a headache. The boys had gone to bed without a murmur, and Mr Cooper had gone up soon afterwards. She liked having the downstairs to herself – she wandered into the front parlour to tidy and check the fire was safe. It was a pretty room, full of knick-knacks and bits and pieces, but not somewhere the boys could play unsupervised without breaking something precious. Satisfied the room was as it should be, she returned to the kitchen.

She was making a shirt for Joe and would finish that before she went upstairs to her attic bedroom. She loved her eyrie at the top of the house, especially the two windows that looked out across the river. She could stand and watch the barges at the quay, the dock workers and the casual labourers hurrying about their daily business. Somehow this made her feel a little closer to her brother Alfie, as he'd left Colchester by boat.

Lost in thought, she was dozing in front of the range when she heard a door bang and hurrying footsteps on the stairs. Instantly alert, she was on her feet when Mr Cooper burst in.

'Maria's taken real badly and I'm going to fetch the doctor. I want you to stay with her whilst I go.'

'Have her pains started, sir? Shall I get things ready?'

He didn't answer, stared at her as if he'd not understood. His face was pale. Something wasn't right; this wasn't a normal labour or he wouldn't be looking so anxious.

'I need to talk to you whilst I get my boots on.'

Sarah handed them to him and shivered. It wasn't the cold that made her tremble. There was something dreadfully wrong – she just knew it.

'It's too soon. The baby's not due for another three weeks and Maria don't have big babies – John was not much bigger than a rabbit and he were full term. She's been poorly these past few days and I reckon that's why it's started.'

'But the baby's been active. She was complaining about being kept awake only yesterday.' She tried to look calm and encouraging, but when her ma had Tommy she'd not been allowed in until afterwards so knew little about what actually happened.

'Mrs Cooper said it might be early this time. A lot of movement, it's a sign of a healthy baby, isn't it?'

He nodded. 'Let's hope so, Sarah. But I'm still getting the doctor. Maria reckons it's a girl this time and if anything happens to the baby she'll take it hard.' He stood up, shrugging on his heavy work coat, tying his muffler around his neck. Then, reaching into a deep pocket, he removed his cap and jammed it on his head. 'I'll be as quick as I can; I'll stop by the midwife's on my way – she lives in St Botolph's Street, so I reckon she'll be here first. The doctor's in Queen Street. It'll take me an hour or more to get there and back. Can you manage on your own?'

'Yes, I'll be fine. I'll wait upstairs. Please take care, Mr Cooper. The roads are slippery – it's freezing again tonight.'

In the bedroom there were several candles burning, but the fire had been allowed to go out. Mrs Cooper was lying propped against the pillows, her cheeks flushed, her hair wet with perspiration.

'Maria, I've come to sit with you whilst Mr Cooper fetches the midwife. How close are your pains? Have your waters broken yet?' This was something she'd heard the midwife ask her mother all those years ago. Giving birth was difficult at the best of times and downright dangerous when the mother was already unwell.

There was no response. Maria's eyes flickered and closed again. Sarah rushed to her side, feeling the unnatural heat radiating from her. The baby was coming, but she'd also got a high fever; this could prove fatal to both her and the infant. More women died from childbed fever than anything else. That was one thing she did know, for Nanny had told her.

Perhaps if she made the room cooler it would help. What they wanted in here was a fresh breeze, not more heat. The window stuck a little, but she managed to force it up and was gratified to feel the temperature drop. She must sponge Maria down. Looking round she saw there was a water jug standing half-full on the washstand.

'I think you need to be cooler, Maria. It'll make you more comfortable.' Again there was no answer. It was going to be a long and difficult night. She prayed the boys slept through; she didn't want them awake if the worst happened.

More than half an hour passed before Maria was able to speak.

Sarah had seen the mound of her stomach contract three times. She thanked God the pains weren't coming any closer together. When they did would be the hardest part. To expel a baby was bad enough at the best of times; it wasn't called labour for nothing. To try and do it when you were desperately ill might well prove too much for both infant and mother.

'Sarah? What're you doing here?' Maria turned her head and seeing the empty space beside her tried to push herself upright, flopping back, too feeble to manage it.

'The boys are fast asleep, and Mr Cooper has gone for the midwife. Your baby's coming and I'm trying to reduce your fever before you have to push.' Ringing out the cloth for the umpteenth time, she wiped her patient's face, glad to see that a combination of fresh air and cold water had brought her skin temperature down to almost normal.

'I'm that thirsty, Sarah love. Could you fetch me a drink?'

'I have some here – I haven't used it all.' She was about to tip some of the water into the glass but stopped. 'I'll go down and get you some that's been boiled, and check on the boys whilst I'm about it.'

The contractions continued at five-minute intervals for another hour, but Maria was a lot better in herself. She couldn't imagine why Mr Cooper was taking so long. The midwife and the doctor must have been out on other calls or one of them would surely have been here by now.

'As you're feeling so much better, Maria, shall I go down and make you a cup of tea?' She crossed the room to close the window before taking the jug and cloth away with her.

* * *

The kettle was hissing over the flames when she heard someone on the cobbles outside. Thank goodness! He was back and he had at least one person with him. The back door opened and two muffled figures stepped in.

'Sarah, how is she? I've got Nurse Digby with me. The doctor's out but his housekeeper's promised to send him as soon as he returns.'

'Her fever's broken, thank God, and the contractions are still five minutes apart. She's sitting up and taking notice now, and has drunk two glasses of water and is asking for tea.'

Nurse Digby removed her cape and bonnet. Sarah was impressed by the woman; she was spotless, her apron pristine, her greying hair neatly coiled at the back of her head. Mr Cooper handed over the carpetbag he'd been carrying for her and she nodded.

'Thank you, Mr Cooper. I can find my way upstairs, and you know what I'll need.'

'Is there anything else you'd like me to do?' Sarah asked.

'I shall examine Mrs Cooper. You look rather young; do you have experience of these matters?' Sarah shook her head. 'In which case, my dear, you will be more use to Mr Cooper. I'm sure he could do with a nice cup of tea; it's fair freezing outside.'

Mr Cooper followed the nurse upstairs. She couldn't remember her stepfather even being on the premises when Tommy was born.

The tea was brewed when he returned looking a deal happier than earlier.

'You did well, Sarah. I can't believe Maria's so much better.' He picked up his mug of tea and drained it in one swallow. 'I could do with some bread and cheese. I'm famished after traipsing around all over Colchester looking for that dratted doctor.'

'It won't take a moment, sir, and there's some rock cakes I baked this morning to have afterwards.'

She was busy in the pantry, on edge for news, but Mrs Digby was still upstairs when she carried in the plate.

'Has Nurse Digby not been down yet? What's keeping her so long?'

'She's thorough, that one. Don't worry, she'll be here soon enough.' He'd finished his meal before they heard footsteps on the stairs. They stood up fearing the worst.

Nurse Digby smiled, and Sarah's fingers unclenched. 'Everything's progressing as it should; Mrs Cooper's still weak after her bout of fever but I'm expecting a happy outcome, although not until the morning.'

'Thank you, I was that worried. Sarah brought the fever down; when I set out to fetch you she was real poorly.' He rubbed his eyes and collapsed back in his chair.

'Would you like a cup of tea, nurse? And what about Mrs Cooper – perhaps she could eat something? She'll need her strength for the morning.'

'That would be nice. I'll be getting back, but I'll not be needing hot water for a few hours yet.'

Maria looked a lot better when Sarah went upstairs with the tea and some dainty cheese sandwiches. 'You're a good girl, Sarah. I bless the day that you moved in with us. I'm feeling stronger now, and the pains are regular, but not getting any closer. The boys all arrived in a rush. I reckon this one's a girl; ladies like to take their time.'

'Try and get some sleep. You'll need to be rested later.'

'Listen to her, nurse; you'd think she'd delivered a dozen babies and her only sixteen years of age.' Maria reached out and squeezed Sarah's hand. 'You run along, love, get some sleep. There'll be plenty to do in the morning.'

'As soon as I have everything prepared for tomorrow, I'll go up – that's if Mr Cooper doesn't object.'

'Course he don't. You get a bit of kip. No point in all of us being awake is there?'

Sarah hesitated outside the door. She'd just check the boys were sound before returning to the kitchen. She found Mr Cooper slumped across the table fast asleep; she left him there and went to her own bed.

11

Sarah was in the kitchen the next morning when the three boys trooped in. Mr Cooper had gone out. She prayed it wasn't to fetch the doctor. She'd already told them the baby was coming, but not how gravely ill their mother was. 'Good morning, you're just in time. I have porridge and fresh bread and butter ready for you.'

'How's Ma? Is the baby here yet?' Joe asked anxiously. 'Do we have to go to school this morning, Sarah?'

Davie shook his head, yawning widely. 'Pa's not here. There's someone upstairs with Ma, but I didn't hear no baby crying.'

'I expect your pa's gone out to stretch his legs. He spent the night in the kitchen.' Should she take the boys or would they be better at home? 'I'll ask your pa about school when he gets back.'

She glanced at the clock and saw it was almost seven, high time for the baby to have been delivered. Something had gone wrong – it must have done. She closed her eyes for a moment to send up a fervent prayer.

'Come along, I'm ready to dish up. Why don't you make some toasted bread this morning? I've got a bowl of dripping from Sunday's roast you can spread on it.'

Her suggestion distracted the boys and, in the excitement of browning the bread on the end of a long fork, they forgot about their father's absence and the lack of a new baby in the house. But she didn't; her thoughts turned constantly to what was taking place upstairs. She wished she knew what was happening.

Mr Cooper returned through the front door and he had someone else with him. He didn't come down to join them in the kitchen. Keeping the children entertained occupied her thoughts, although her eyes kept turning anxiously to the clock. The hands moved remorselessly around and still there was no news. School had been abandoned this morning.

At nine o'clock someone left the house. What was going on up there? If it was bad news perhaps Mr Cooper would wish to tell her first.

'I'm going to take some tea upstairs. Behave yourselves whilst I'm gone.' She smiled at Joe. 'I'm relying on you – you're in charge.'

She hesitated in the small vestibule at the bottom of the stairs. The cups rattled on their saucers. The thin wail of a baby filtered through the floorboards. Thank God! The baby was alive. Mr Cooper must be upstairs admiring the new arrival. He appeared looking drawn, but smiling.

'It's a girl. It was touch-and-go, but everything's fine now. Maria can't wait to show you the baby. Is that tea you have there? I'm coming down. I'll have mine in the kitchen with the boys; give them the good news.'

'I'm so glad for you. Have the nurse and doctor gone? Were there complications?'

'You'd better ask Maria. All I know is, I'm glad it's over.' He rubbed his eyes. For the first time since she'd met him he was unshaven. 'We've got our daughter now – there'll be no more. I'm not having her go through that again.' He stepped round her, removing a cup and saucer from the tray as he passed. He didn't seem overjoyed at the arrival of the much-longed-for girl.

Maria was lying propped up in bed, looking exhausted but radiant, the infant cradled in her arms. 'I'm so glad everything turned out well. I've brought you and Nurse Digby a cup of tea. Shall I bring it in?'

The midwife bustled over. 'Good girl. Exactly what Mrs Cooper needs and I must say a cup of tea will do me good as well.'

Sarah put the tray down and took a cup over to the bed.

'Would you like to hold her, Sarah? I daren't drink tea with her in my arms.'

The baby was so small, and there was a strange blue tint around her mouth. She stroked the baby's velvet cheek, tears pricking at the backs of her eyes. She could recall holding Tommy in just this way when he'd been only an hour or so old. This baby seemed so tiny by comparison. Perhaps they'd got their dates wrong. It often happened. 'What are you going to call her? Have you decided?'

'Emily. It was my own ma's name. What do you think?'

'I think it's lovely, and so's she.'

Maria patted the empty side of the bed and Sarah sat down beside her, dismayed to see the flush across Maria's cheeks – the fever had returned. She didn't like to suggest the window was opened, not with the new baby.

'Mr Cooper's telling the boys. They'll want to see you and Emily. Are you up to a visit?'

'Of course I am. They'll be as pleased as punch. Did Dan tell you what happened – why we had to send for the doctor?'

Sarah would prefer not to know the details. It wasn't her place to be told such things. 'No, I gather there were complications.'

'She was a breech delivery; if she'd been any bigger I reckon neither of us would have survived. The doctor couldn't turn her, and I've got a lot of stitches, but we're both here. I'm going to need you to help with Emily this next week, Sarah love.'

'I'll be thrilled. I don't have enough to do as it is; Joe and Davie are at school of a morning, and John's no trouble. Nelly does all the hard work round here.'

The boys, once they were sure their ma was well, took little interest in the baby. Mr Cooper went back to work. He couldn't take further time off or he'd have his wages docked. His position was a responsible one and he took his duties seriously.

It was left to her to change the baby and launder the rags used to keep her backside clean. Maria still had a fever, but she insisted it was only a bit of a cold and she'd be right as ninepence in no time at all. It was the baby Sarah was most concerned about. Emily was too quiet, was a poor feeder and didn't seem to be thriving the way Tommy had.

Mr Cooper didn't come in any more to eat with the boys; when he returned at lunchtimes he got on with some project in the capacious shed at the bottom of the yard. She was obliged to take his soup and sandwich out to him. However, he always went upstairs to greet his wife and see the baby before he went back to work. Did he realise there was something not quite right with Emily? Was that why he was so distant? If the baby was ailing surely he would send for the doctor?

* * *

A few days later Sarah took the midday meal upstairs as usual. Maria was tossing about restlessly on the bed, her breathing harsh. Her fever hadn't returned; it was something different this time. She almost dropped the tray. 'Mrs Cooper, Maria, what is it? You should have banged on the floor. I'd have come up straightaway.'

'I feel right poorly, Sarah. My leg hurts something rotten and I can't catch my breath.'

'I'll fetch Mr Cooper. He's in the yard.'

She fled through the kitchen, ignoring the open mouths of the boys. Something was dreadfully wrong. Mr Cooper must run and fetch the doctor. He looked up from his carpentry.

'The baby?'

'No, sir, it's Mrs Cooper. I don't know what's wrong. She's desperately ill. Please come at once.'

He took one look at his wife and his face paled. 'Maria, Sarah will sit with you and Emily. I'll fetch the doctor. He'll soon sort you out. Don't fret, love. You rest quiet until I get back.'

It could be an hour or more before he returned. She had to trust the boys not to do anything silly in her absence; she daren't leave Maria on her own. All she could do was hold the patient's hand and murmur nonsense to her, but it seemed to help. She'd been sitting by the bed for half an hour when the door opened slowly and Joe's face peeped round.

'Is Ma poorly, Sarah?'

She hurried over to him, hoping he hadn't seen his mother's struggle to breathe. 'Yes, Joe, I'm afraid she is. Can you be a big boy and take care of your brothers for me? I have to stay here until your pa gets back.'

'I can do that. We can play spillikins – Davie and John like that.'

'Good boy.' She gathered him close, kissing his curls, praying he wouldn't have to cope with the misery of losing his beloved mother. 'You can get down the biscuit tin. You may have two each. Make sure you put the lid on tight after, won't you?'

His worried frown vanished at the promised treat. Biscuits were only for Sundays. 'I will. We'll be quiet as mice, then Ma can have a nice rest.'

It was a further dragging twenty minutes before the front door opened and help arrived. It wasn't the doctor who had come back with Mr Cooper.

She smiled encouragingly at Maria. 'Mrs Digby's here now. She'll know what to do.' Sarah was relieved to leave the patient in expert hands.

'If you would care to wait downstairs, Mr Cooper; I'll call if I need you. Doctor Andrews will be here at any moment.'

He followed Sarah out of the sickroom. He gestured for her to accompany him to the parlour and closed the door behind them. 'Sarah, Emily is as sick as Maria. The doctor told me she has a heart condition, will not live much longer.'

'I thought she was too quiet; if anything happens to the baby, Mrs Cooper will be heartbroken.'

'That's why I haven't told her. I wanted her to be stronger before I broke the news.' His throat convulsed, and he brushed his hand across his eyes. 'I'm trusting you to take care of my boys; whatever happens today they'll need you more than ever. You're like a second mother to them already. Get them ready and take them for a walk along the river. I don't want them here this afternoon.'

He expected his wife to die. Sarah couldn't speak, feared she would break down if she tried. She had to be strong. Now was not the time to give in. He didn't require an answer, merely nodded and patted her shoulder, then with heavy feet returned to his wife. Pinning on a false smile she joined the children.

Joe looked up from the game. 'I saw the doctor go in a while back. That's a good thing, ain't it, Sarah?'

'I'm sure it is, Joe. Now, I thought we could go and feed the ducks.

Davie, can you fetch your coats and mufflers from the scullery? Joe, will you and John bring in the boots?'

With a basket of stale bread over one arm, and John's hand in the other, she took them away as instructed. In spite of the sun it was cold by the river. Even the ducks seemed dispirited. It was no good; she couldn't keep them out any longer.

'Sarah, John's wet himself. He never asked like what he normally does.'

She scooped the miserable child into her arms. 'Never mind, sweetheart, accidents happen. Let's get back into the warm and I'll put nice dry clothes on you.'

They'd been away almost two hours. The clock had just struck three. Joe carried the empty basket; Davie held his other hand. John grizzled all the way back. The house was quiet, too quiet. She stripped off his wet clothes and replaced them with the fresh that were kept downstairs for such an eventuality. She got down the Snap cards and found them a barley twist to suck before going to investigate. She could hear someone in the parlour. She tapped on the door. Mr Cooper opened it; his face was ravaged, his eyes tear-filled. He shook his head and turned away to continue his pacing back and forth.

Sarah rushed upstairs dreading what she'd find. Nurse Digby was bending over, a still figure in the bed. She didn't need to ask – Maria was dead.

The nurse straightened, her eyes glittering. 'Mrs Cooper seemed better. Her breathing was easier and she fed the infant. I was changing the baby when she suddenly collapsed. It was a congestion of the lungs. It's not uncommon when a new mother has been poorly.'

Sarah could hardly take it in. The three boys were motherless. How would Mr Cooper manage on his own? She walked over to the bed – forced herself to look for the last time. Maria's face was already cold as a marble slab, and as white. What she must have suffered to have died like this.

The nurse sniffed and dried her eyes. 'Doctor Andrews will call in at the vicarage on his way home. I shall stop by the undertaker's...' The woman looked uncomfortable and cleared her throat before continuing.

'The baby will be joining her any time now. I'm surprised she has survived so long.'

Poor Mr Cooper, to lose his wife and infant on the same day. 'How long?' She couldn't manage any more, hardly dared look in the cradle.

'This evening – no longer than that. I'm glad Mrs Cooper didn't know about the baby. They'll be together in heaven soon.'

Sarah wasn't certain about that. But they'd be together in a coffin – that's for sure. Leaving the midwife to do what was necessary she slipped out. She braced herself against the wall, forcing down her grief. This family needed her. She must hold firm for their sake. They'd taken her in when she'd been desperate; she must do everything she could to help the boys and Mr Cooper come to terms with the double tragedy.

Downstairs she discovered him slumped in an armchair, his shoulders no longer heaving, but shudders travelled up and down his spine at intervals. What he needed was a strong mug of tea with plenty of sugar. He would have to pull himself together; he needed to tell his sons before the undertakers appeared. He must know about the imminent demise of the baby. Was he delaying things until he could give them both pieces of bad news?

The children were sitting round the table playing Snap. It was the quietest game she'd heard them play. 'I'm making a nice cup of tea. I'm sure you could do with one to warm you up after our long walk.'

Fortunately they were too engrossed to ask questions. She placed a mug of milky tea in front of each boy and then carried another into the front room. This time she didn't knock.

'Here you are, Mr Cooper, drink this. Maria needs you to be strong. The boys have to be told and arrangements made. I can't do it for you.'

He pushed himself upright rubbing his face on his sleeve, not bothering to reach for his handkerchief. His eyes were red and puffy, his nose running. He had to get himself straight before he could go next door. She handed him the damp cloth she'd had the foresight to bring with her. Like an automaton he cleaned his face and took a few slurps from his mug.

'Thank God you're here, Sarah. The boys will not take it so hard having you to comfort them. I'll go and tell them. Will you come with me?'

'I'm going to hold Emily. She can't be allowed to die on her own.' Not waiting for his response she went back to the bedroom. The midwife had finished laying out the body. Maria looked as if she was sleeping now, her arms folded across her chest, a fresh nightgown on and her hair neatly braided. It was kind of Nurse Digby to do this for them – Sarah wasn't sure it was usually her task.

'I thought I'd sit and hold the baby...' She couldn't continue, couldn't ask what she should do when the child drew her last breath.

'You're a good girl, Sarah. Just place the baby in her arms when she's gone. I've left room for her. Doctor Andrews will be along later to write the death certificates. I'll see myself out. It's a very sad day, but Mrs Cooper told me she knew you would take care of her family when she'd gone. There's not many women can pass over confident of that.'

The room was silent and unpleasantly cold. She supposed it made no sense to waste coal. She reached into the cradle and picked up the infant. She placed one finger on Emily's tiny cheek; it was still warm. She was glad the little one wouldn't die alone.

Downstairs the boys were crying, Mr Cooper consoling them. It was better they were with their father. She rocked the bundle gently, murmuring words of love, telling the baby she would soon be with her mother in heaven. After a while she loosened the shawl and reached in to take the baby's hand. Maybe physical touch would give her comfort in her final hours.

It was dark in the room when she realised she was holding Emily's mortal remains. The baby had died as quietly as she'd lived. Dry-eyed she wrapped the little body up and carried it across to place it gently in Maria's arms where she belonged.

It was quiet downstairs. She daren't cry. The loss was too great; if she let down her defences for a second she would be overcome. Maria was relying on her, but it was a heavy burden on someone not yet seventeen years of age. She was committed to the Cooper family. She must forget all hope of joining Alfie or setting up in a business of her own. Sarah had

dreamed of having her own dressmaking business one day, but that must
be forgotten as her life was now here.

12

LONDON, MAY 1844

'Have you got your ticket for tomorrow, Alfie?'

'I got it this morning. You know, George, the bugger made me pay the same for Buster. He ain't going to sit on the seat; he'll go under it. It's a blooming cheek making me pay twice.'

The dog, hearing his name, got up from the cobbles and wandered over, shoving his huge head under Alfie's arm slopping his tea over his trousers. 'Get on with you, stupid animal. Good job we're outside in the yard. George wouldn't be best pleased if we got it all over his clean floor.'

'I reckon we've made a good job of this cottage, Alfie. It's a regular little home from home; my girl's coming to see it tomorrow. It's a shame you won't be here to meet her.'

'I'm catching the first train from Bishopsgate Street station. I need to get to Colchester in plenty of time. I want to find meself a bed for the night and then have a look round for somewhere permanent to rent.' He drained his mug and set it down on the windowsill. He was more than ready to leave the city. Already the stench was worse even though the choking smog had eased as people burnt less coal.

'Still, we've got this evening to spend together. I'm taking you for a slap-up meal and no arguments. I couldn't have got the place ready if you hadn't moved in with me like what you did.'

'Happy to do it. That's what mates are for, ain't they? Moving here saved me the rent on the room for a couple of months and I've learnt a whole lot more about this carpentry business. Them tables I made last week were a bit of all right, weren't they?'

His friend grinned. 'I reckon you're more than ready to set up on your own; if you stick to tables, benches and dressers you'll have no complaints.' George collected the empty mugs and turned to go indoors. 'The water will be hot enough for us to have our bath. If you finish putting things away out here, I'll get myself washed and then it'll be your turn.'

'Well, Buster, we'll be smart as paint tomorrow. You with your fine collar and lead, and me all spruced up in me best togs. You'll love the country, you wait and see.'

* * *

It was a fair old walk from George's drum to the station so Alfie left at sunrise. He paused as he turned out of the yard. He doubted he'd ever see his friend again. He had no intention of coming back to London; he'd done with it now. If Jim hadn't died, things would have been different.

Buster had become accustomed to being led and made no protest when he clipped the lead to his collar. The dog in one hand, his carpetbag in the other, he headed for the east side of London. He wasn't too sure about going back in that direction; it had unpleasant memories for him, but that's where the train left for Colchester so he had no choice.

Bishopsgate Street station was like a place from hell. The clanking and groaning of the massive steam engines, the shouts, wails and whistles from the guards, made him wish he'd decided to travel all the way on foot. Buster shivered at his side. He hoped the dog would consent to getting on the train when the time came to embark.

He reached into his waistcoat pocket and withdrew his two tickets. There were three classes: first for the toffs, second for the middling folk and third class for the likes of him and Buster. The carriage was open to the elements, sides and seats the only comfort provided. If it rained he'd be drenched, but he weren't spending his hard-earned cash to sit inside.

He could imagine the uproar if Buster farted; no he was better off in the fresh air.

His seat was towards the end of the train. There were already a handful of passengers ahead of him. He was relieved he didn't have to take his dog any closer to the hissing engine – he'd never have got him aboard then. He found his allotted space and Buster needed no encouragement to wriggle under the seat. Amazing how small he could make himself when he tried.

Promptly at seven o'clock the guard blew his whistle and waved his green flag. The train shuddered and heaved and rumbled forward. After a few miles the novelty of travelling at such speed wore off. His arse was black and blue from being bounced up and down on the hard seat and he was covered in soot from the engine's smoke. He'd look like Black Ben by the time he arrived.

For all that, it was nothing short of miraculous travelling fifty miles in less than two hours. It would have taken him all day in the mail coach and three days to walk. Being covered in soot and having a sore arse seemed a small price to pay when he stepped onto the platform of Colchester station. He glanced around. It weren't up to much, not much more than a wooden shed really.

He was back home. Nearly three years had gone by since he'd left with that bastard captain. He'd been a boy then; he was returning a man. This had nothing to do with age; he'd taken care of himself, learnt a decent trade and come back with his waistcoat filled with five-pound notes. Ma would be proud of him. Even Jack Rand would think twice about knocking him about.

His lips curved. It were Sarah he wanted to see. She'd not recognise him, but then she'd have changed as well. He'd find himself a billet for the night, somewhere at the bottom of North Hill, then he'd cut along the river and up to Maidenburgh Street. It was there he was going to look for a cottage to rent. It was a stone's throw to the water meadows where Buster could roam around freely.

Like the other passengers he took a few moments to bang the worst of the city smuts from his person. Buster, who had spent the entire journey cowering under the seat, was relatively clean. 'Are you ready,

Buster? This is where I come from. It's going to be our home from now on.'

'That's a fine dog you have there, mister; don't see many as big as him round here.' The speaker was a young man not much older than himself, similarly dressed, an almost identical carpetbag under his arm.

'I've been away a few years. Are you local, then?' The man followed him down the slope to the road that would lead them into Colchester.

'I am. Sam Foster's the name, been up the Smoke on business.' Foster fell into step beside him.

'Alfie Nightingale, and this here's Buster. I've been working in the city, made enough to set meself up in a little business. What line of work you in?'

'Family business; we buy and sell, and lend a bit to those who need it.'

'I'm a carpenter by trade, and aim to run a delivery service along with that.' They were over the bridge at the bottom of North Hill. 'I'm turning off here. Good to meet you, Sam.'

'Good luck to you, Alfie. I drink at The Red Lion most nights; maybe I'll see you there?' He tipped his cap and strode off.

The kind of business Sam Foster was involved in sounded like the same kind of business Silas Field had run. He didn't look Jewish – if he had, he would have supposed his pa to be an *uncle*, to run a pop shop. It weren't any of his business, but he'd make sure he stayed away from The Red Lion, find somewhere else to wet his whistle.

As soon as he was along the river path he released the dog. 'Go on, old fellow, have a sniff about. This is your patch now.' The dog didn't dash off as he was wont to do, but hovered nervously a few yards from him. Alfie smiled; this was the first time in the two years they'd been together he'd seen Buster unsure of himself. 'It's countryside, Buster, it won't hurt you. Go and have a look-see – find yourself a coney.'

They met no one in the water meadows; it could have been in the depths of the country not on the outskirts of a bustling market town. Alfie leant against the stile that separated the fields from the path that led to the bottom of the street where he hoped to find a vacant cottage. The clean air and early summer sunshine refreshed him. He was confident he'd made the right decision.

'Buster, time to go. Better put your lead back on; don't want people to be put off when we're looking for somewhere to stay tonight.' The dog had soon got over his anxiety and had spent the past half-hour galloping through the grass, barking at any wildfowl he came across. He turned towards the area of Colchester he'd grown up in. It was only then he recalled he'd just walked past the stretch of river where his little brother had drowned. He'd all but forgotten that tragedy. He'd been a different person then; it was in the past.

* * *

The very next day he found what he was looking for. The man what owned the place was a Mr Hatch. He was to meet him that afternoon to seal the deal.

'This will suit me fine. I'll take it. Three months in advance do you, Mr Hatch?'

'Let's shake on it, Mr Nightingale. Pleasure to do business with you. The outbuildings need a bit of doing up, but being a carpenter, that'll be no problem to you. The kitchen range was installed this year. Most of the furniture is in good order. You've paid a fair price for it. If you need anything else, you know where to find me.' Money exchanged hands and Alfie had his first rent book. One day he'd have the deeds to a property in his hand, be beholden to no one, but this was a good start.

He'd only given the place a quick glance-over to know it was perfect for him. The previous tenants had left the place clean; although sparsely furnished, what was there would do him for the moment. It was a bit more than he'd intended to pay, but when he'd seen the yard and the row of dilapidated sheds he'd known it was ideal. It was at the end of the terrace, the back gate opening onto the path that led down to the river.

He hadn't thought he'd find something as quickly. He'd only had to spend one night in a lodging house. Rattling the two keys, he called the dog to his side. 'Buster, come and see our new home. You can go out again later once we're settled.'

The landlord had left the place unlocked. Alfie hung the keys on the hook inside the back door, tossing his carpetbag onto the kitchen table.

The range was the same as the one they'd had in East Stockwell Street. Many's the time he'd had to light that for his ma. Then he examined it more closely. It weren't the same. It had no open grate, the fire was behind a metal door, and there was a place to put your pots and pans to heat up. He saw a small brass tap poking out of the metal. He turned it without thinking.

'Bleedin' hell! Would you look at that, Buster? I've got a boot full of water. I reckon when this is lit we'll have hot water to wash in whenever we like.'

He must stop talking to his dog as if he were a human. He needed a mate, someone to share his life with, someone like Jim. No, he'd not want a friend again; what he wanted was a family of his own. He'd go and see Ma tomorrow, find out where his Sarah was, try and persuade her to move into his cottage. Then they could start a life together like what they'd always planned to do. He weren't ready to find himself a sweetheart; that was for the future. What he needed was company of a night. Who better than his sister?

His home had a good-sized scullery attached to the left of the kitchen. Although it had a door into the yard this had to be unbolted from the inside. The kitchen had shelves either side of the range, more than adequate for his needs. There was a table, not as good as he could make himself, and two chairs. The door to the right of the range opened inwards. There was a tiny hallway, with the stairs leading up to the two bedrooms. He crossed the hall in one stride and entered the front room. This opened onto Maidenburgh Street. Being at the bottom of the hill it didn't require more than a single step outside.

The room was a decent size, had a fireplace, a stone mantelshelf above it and a window overlooking the road. There were boards on the floor, but no furniture. He'd purchase himself a rug, a comfy armchair and make himself a side table to put an oil lamp on. He'd not use this room until Sarah came; then she could furnish it the way *she* wanted.

The stairs, although steep, were straight. A matching hallway at the top; to the left a bedroom above the kitchen, to the right a bedroom above the parlour. Both had bed frames, washstands and hooks to hang his clothes. He chose the one at the back; it would be quieter and gave him an unrestricted view of the yard.

When he'd got a couple of handcarts out there he'd want to be sure no one stole them. His years of living in London had made him wary. Hadn't the very first person he'd met been someone outside the law? Colchester was no better than anywhere else in that respect – there were always folk ready to steal instead of work.

* * *

He'd get himself settled; buy what he needed and stock up his larder before taking himself round to his old home. It was too hot for his tweed suit; he'd put on a clean shirt and his spare trousers. His hair was clean. He'd got George to trim it the other night, and he'd not had crawlers since he'd parted company with Ginger and the gang.

There were pots and pans, crockery and cutlery on the shelves now. He'd bought a meat safe, put it in the scullery and covered it with a wet cloth. His milk, butter and cheese should stay fresh enough like that. He'd not bothered to light the range, but it was laid and ready, the coal he'd ordered safely stored in the one shed with a decent lock on the door. His position on the end of the row meant he didn't have to share his privy with anyone, but he still had to go into his neighbour's yard to get his water. At least what he pumped up was fresh enough to drink, not like the pumps where he'd been living.

'You stop here, Buster; take care of things for me. Your water's by the back step, and you got your bone to chew on. I don't think Ma's ready to meet you straight off.'

He locked the kitchen door and put the key behind a loose brick in the wall of the scullery. He'd no worries about being burgled, not when his dog was in the yard. The key were too cumbersome to lug around with him. He'd find somewhere better to hide it later.

The walk up the hill to the High Street took him five minutes longer than usual, for he stopped every few yards to stare. Everything looked exactly as it had when he'd left three years ago. He was the one who'd changed, not Colchester. He stepped into the High Street and gawped.

Crickey! There must have been a fire at the far end. He crossed the road, standing outside The Red Lion in order to get a proper look. St Peter's Vicarage had gone and there was a smart new building in its place.

He dodged back between the hackney carriages, the diligences and private vehicles and entered East Stockwell Street, surprised how nervous he felt. The house he'd lived in most of his life was a third of the way down, the end of a row of ancient cottages. Should he go round the back, or knock on the front door? He'd do neither. He'd call at Mrs Sainty's, see how the land lay before he risked a confrontation with his stepfather.

Shuffling footsteps approached, bolts were drawn back and then the door opened. She hadn't changed, still as stout and dishevelled as ever. 'Can I help you, young sir?'

'It's me, Alfie, Mrs Sainty. I'm back to find my Sarah.'

Her eyes widened, she clutched the doorjamb for support. 'Good God! I never knew you, Alfie. You're a real toff now, made your fortune in the city did you?' She stepped to one side.

'You come along in. I've got the kettle on. Things have changed around here. I'm glad you called here first.'

By the time she'd finished he was as dumbfounded as she'd been earlier. Fancy Ma doing a vanishing act, not bothering to tell his sister she was going. 'Has Sarah been around lately?'

'I've not seen her since, let me see, spring last year. She's too busy, I reckon, what with her promotion and all. You go on round to Grey Friars House, let her know you're back. She was that desperate when you didn't return. Imagine, working on a coal barge all those months.' She smiled and prodded his arm. 'That's where you got those muscles from, so it weren't all bad news.'

'And your boys, what are they doing with themselves nowadays?'

'Bert's taken the Queen's shilling and George's moved in with his fancy woman on Balkerne Hill.'

'Maybe I'll look him up now I'm back.'

'Promise me you'll come round and see me, give us news of Sarah won't you, Alfie?'

'I will, Mrs Sainty. I'm going round right away to Grey Friars.'

No time like the present; he couldn't wait to see his sister's face. Would she be as shocked as Mrs Sainty to see the change in him? His old neigh-bour had told him Sarah was a young lady now, head nursemaid at this grand house. It was good news for her, but he doubted she'd want to leave her position to join him in Maidenburgh Street.

He'd not ask her to until his business was prospering and he had a steady income. She could do a bit of sewing – she was always good with a needle – make herself some extra. He didn't want her to work in a factory, do something menial. He wanted to provide for her, give her the little luxuries she'd never had. There was no point in having all this money if he couldn't share it with someone else.

The sound of voices coming from the coach house behind Grey Friars House attracted him. He'd ask whoever it was in there if he could speak to Sarah. He didn't fancy knocking on the door – they might send him away without asking him his business. Grand folks didn't take too kindly to people like him banging on their back doors uninvited.

A girl, her blonde hair neatly coiled at the back of her neck, had her back to him as she was talking to a groom. Her smart grey dress told him she was a senior servant. His Sarah would be a senior too.

'Excuse me, miss, I'm looking for Sarah Nightingale. I was told my sister worked here.'

She spun, and smiled at him as if he was a long-lost friend. 'Alfie, you've come back at last. Sarah's not working here any more. I can't tell you how glad I am to see you. Can you come back tomorrow at two o'clock? I have the afternoon off and I can explain everything to you then.'

Too stunned to do more than nod, he watched the girl run lightly back towards the house. He didn't want to talk to the groom; he needed to get away, try and understand what the girl had said. He didn't even know her name. She must be a friend of Sarah's to know all about *him*. Somehow he was back on the pathway walking the wrong way, down the hill instead of back past the castle.

Ma gone, and now Sarah – he couldn't believe he'd come back to find his family scattered. He was more alone here than he'd been in London, for at least there he'd had George's companionship.

13

COLCHESTER, MAY 1844

'When Mr and Mrs Davies come, I thought we'd take a picnic along the riverbank for a change. What do you think boys?'

Joe paused in the game of marbles he was playing with Davie. 'We ain't been on a picnic in years, Sarah – perhaps Pa will come with us?'

'I don't know about that, Joe. He's very busy at the moment.' There was a tug on her skirt.

'He don't go to work on Sundays, do he, Sarah? So where's he gone then?'

'I expect there's something special he had to do. Remember your father has a very important position at the timber yard. It's his hard work that gives us all the extras we wouldn't have otherwise. Now, who's going to go and get the eggs from the chicken run for me?'

Joe and Davie ran off, a basket held between them, leaving her alone with John. She crouched down beside him, quickly collecting up the little painted clay balls and returning them to the cloth bag. She didn't trust the child not to push one up his nose or try to swallow it. 'Come along, young man, you can measure the ingredients and mix up the sponge cake.'

After settling him on the chair beside her, she handed him a pudding basin and wooden spoon. There was no need to weigh the butter or flour. She'd made scones so many times she could do it blindfold. The sponge cake also; she used her ma's recipe – a cupful of each ingredient two eggs and a little milk.

The weeks had slipped past since that dreadful day. The first two weeks had been the worst, John wetting the bed every night, Joe calling out every half an hour for her to come. Stumbling up and down the attic stairs so often she was surprised she hadn't broken her neck.

One afternoon she came back from a walk to find everything had changed. Dan had been sleeping in the parlour; now his bed was in the attic along with his clothes. Her rickety bed frame was in the marital bedroom with all her belongings. He'd left the drawers, the commode, washstand and clothes cupboard for her use.

He said the children needed her close by; he didn't want to sleep in the room his wife and baby had died in, so it was the perfect solution. He'd packed away Maria's ornaments and knick-knacks. The front room was for the boys in future. They could play in there, get out from under her feet whilst she was working.

John rapped her on the knuckles with his spoon. 'Sarah, what I do next?'

Laughing, she tipped the beaten eggs into the cake mix. 'Sorry, sweetheart, I was wool-gathering. There, you stir, and I'll help you put it in the tins. Your brothers are back with the rest of the eggs. We're going to hard-boil those to take on the picnic.'

Mrs Davies and her husband had been coming every Sunday for lunch or tea since she'd moved in here. It was Dan's suggestion. She treasured the afternoons she spent in the company of the old folk. It was hard to make friends when you didn't get any time off. She couldn't even go and see Betty, but Dan kept insisting she wasn't an employee but a member of the family.

She wasn't entirely comfortable with this new arrangement as it meant she was tied indefinitely to the Cooper household. Didn't he realise one day she might wish to leave, to get married and set up a home of her own? Or maybe he'd wish to find himself another wife. The next Mrs Cooper wouldn't take kindly to a servant being treated like a blood relative. Whatever he said, she *was* still a servant and didn't want it any other way.

He still gave her far more than she needed for housekeeping, told her to put anything left over in her savings account for a rainy day. Maybe this was his way of saying he understood that one day she would leave, but not yet. The children must come first at the moment.

The food was packed, two rugs rolled up and ready when the visitors arrived. John greeted the elderly couple with the news they were going on a picnic.

'My word! We ain't been on one of them since I don't know when. It'll be a rare treat being out in the fresh air on a lovely day like this. What have we got in this here picnic then, young John?'

The children listed the contents of the two baskets and the elderly couple exclaimed appropriately. Sarah was returning from the privy with John when Dan returned.

'We're going on a picnic, Pa,' Joe shouted. 'You can come with us, can't you?' The child grabbed Dan's hand. Sarah held her breath, praying he would agree. He glanced up, catching her eye, then grinned and nodded.

'I wouldn't miss it for the world, son. A picnic's just what we need on a day like this. Give us a minute to change out of me work clothes and I'll be ready to come with you.' He ruffled the boy's hair. 'You and Davie fetch your ball. We can have a kick-about if we can find somewhere safe.'

She knew he was referring to her brother Tommy. She'd told the children about this in order to stop them running too close to the bank on their frequent walks by the water.

* * *

When they returned John was asleep, his head lolling on his father's shoulder. Mrs Davies carried the empty baskets and her husband the rugs. Sarah walked with Joe and Davie. Even they were subdued, the fresh air and riotous game of football having tired them out. They said farewell to the old couple outside the house. She hoped they'd manage the long trek up the hill to their own cottage without mishap.

She unlocked the back door, Dan standing beside her. 'I'll give you a hand putting this lot to bed. I reckon you'll not hear a peep from them tonight. About time you got a good night's rest.'

'Thank you, Dan. We'll just take their clothes off. I'm not bothering to wash them all over tonight, just a quick wipe with a wet flannel will have to do.'

Between them this task was accomplished smoothly. He patted her shoulder. 'I'll get the kettle on, Sarah. We could both do with a cup of tea.'

He clattered down to the kitchen, leaving her to give them a final goodnight kiss. They were all asleep before she left the room. She removed her boots and bonnet, slipping on her indoor shoes. These were another little extra Dan had insisted she bought. Her cupboard was full of gowns, shawls and petticoats; why, she even had *two* bonnets now!

He was too generous. It wasn't right for him to treat her like this. She feared she was becoming more and more beholden. Tonight she'd explain how she felt, get things back on a more formal footing. It would make things easier later. She hadn't given up hope that Alfie would come back for her one day.

The kitchen was empty. He must be locking up the chickens. The tea was brewing, the milk, sugar and two cups waiting on the table. With the window and back door left open, the heat from the range wasn't too bad. Her rocking chair was by the open door most evenings. Listening to the nightingales was a treat after a long day's work. Usually Dan sat in the parlour reading the paper. This was the first time since Maria's death they'd spent any time together.

His shirt glowed white in the darkness as he returned from the far end of the yard. 'That broody hen has a clutch of chicks under her. They must have hatched today. The boys will be excited when they see them tomorrow.'

'She was sitting on more than a dozen. I wonder how many will be hens.'

'It don't matter either way – the cockerels make good eating.' He collected his tea from the table and brought a chair to join hers. 'I enjoyed myself today, Sarah, thank you for arranging it. You're a good girl. Maria would be happy to know you're here being a mother to her boys.'

Her cup rattled against the saucer. She placed it down beside her. Keeping her head lowered she had to explain. 'It's not right, treating me as one of the family. I'm not a relative; I'm an employee. One day you'll want to get married again and your next wife will not take kindly to this arrangement. I might even want to get married myself. What then?'

She raised her head, daring to look at him. He wasn't angry or offended; there was a faint gleam of something she half-recognised in his eyes.

'You're quite right to remind me, Sarah. I'll not say it to the boys any more. But you're a friend, I hope, not just an employee.'

'Dan, it's an honour to call myself your friend. I'm glad you understand my position. I don't want there to be any misunderstanding in the future.'

He grinned. For some reason her cheeks coloured. 'Sarah, is there something you've not told me? Do you have someone in mind?'

She frowned, not understanding.

'A young man? Are you leaving to get married soon?'

'I should think not. I'm not seventeen until October, far too young to be thinking about that sort of to-do.'

'Promise me you won't leave for any other reason and I'll be content.'

'I promise. I'm very happy here and I love the boys.'

'Good. Now, Joe and Davie have their birthdays at the beginning of August, and John will be four in July. Let's have a party to celebrate their anniversaries. Maria wouldn't want us to grieve any more. It will be nearly six months by then. Time to move on. Don't you agree?'

'I suppose so, and the boys would love it. Do you mean a *real* party? One with cake and guests and party games? I've never even been to a party, let alone arranged one.' She smiled, that wasn't quite true. 'Although I did attend one when I was working as a nursemaid.'

'In which case, you're the expert. Can you make a birthday cake, buy the extras and things? We must think about gifts as well.'

She yawned, covering her mouth apologetically. 'Of course I can, but not now – we've months to plan it. I think I'll retire, Dan. It's been a long day and all the fresh air has quite worn me out.' She stood up, ready to do her usual chores, but he shook his head.

'No, you go on up, Sarah. I'll do what's necessary.'

It was some time before she could settle in spite of her fatigue. Had she said enough? Did Dan understand her position? He'd seemed unperturbed by her request, not at all upset by her suggestion that one day she would be leaving. She had no intention of getting married yet.

Unless he found himself a wife she'd be quite content to stay where she was. But she wished she hadn't made that promise. If Alfie came back, things might be different then. But why should she live with her brother when she had such a good position here? Whatever he might offer couldn't possibly match what she already had in comfort and security.

* * *

Alfie spent far longer on his appearance than was customary. He checked his cravat was neatly tied, shirt clean and waistcoat unstained. He gave a last rub to his boots confident they couldn't be any shinier. Today he wore his jacket, a bit warm for anything apart from shirtsleeves, but he intended to make a good impression. He'd thought of little else but the girl he'd met briefly the day before. She was small, barely came up to his shoulder, but her pale blue eyes sparkled and her blonde hair had shone around her face.

Leaving Buster at home, he set off up the hill taking a shortcut around the bailey of the castle. He waited opposite the rear entrance to Grey Friars. The church on the hill struck two. Moments later the girl emerged. He caught his breath. She was even lovelier than he'd remembered. Out of uniform today, her pretty straw bonnet caught his eye. Her dress, in a soft pink material, fitted snugly over the finest bosom he'd ever seen.

He was about to cross the road when she waved back, then dodged expertly in and out of the traffic to arrive laughing and breathless at his side. 'You must think me daft, Alfie Nightingale. Inviting myself to meet you and you not knowing who I am.' She dipped in a mock curtsy. 'I'm Betty Thomas.'

Laughing, he bowed solemnly. 'Pleased to meet you, Betty Thomas. I'm desperate to know what happened to Sarah. Let's find somewhere quiet we can talk.'

It wouldn't be proper to invite her back to the cottage, be on their own like; he didn't know much about how things were done, but being alone with a girl wasn't something he'd suggest so early in their acquaintance.

'I know somewhere in Wire Street, Mr Doe's Temperance Hotel – we'll go there. You look the kind of gent who can afford to take a girl out for a cup of tea.' Without being asked, she placed her arm in his. 'Mind you, we can find a wall to sit on if you ain't comfortable going to a place like that.'

'No, much better inside where we can get a bit of privacy.' He marched off, following her directions, feeling ten feet tall. He'd never been in a hotel, so left matters in her capable hands.

The waitress ushered them to a quiet corner. Betty ordered tea and cakes. He waited for the girl to leave before asking about his sister. For some reason he'd not wanted to spoil the mood on the walk through Colchester.

'Now, what happened? Why were Sarah turned off?'

'In a minute, Alfie. First I've got something to give you; she left this with me. I've other things of hers, books and such. Next time we meet I'll give them to you.'

He wasn't sure he liked being ordered about by this slip of a girl. Maybe she felt superior because she was a bit older than him. He'd not bother at the moment, but it would be best to put her straight when they met again.

She put a small white parcel on the tablecloth. He raised his eyebrows; she said nothing. He unfolded the material and his eyes filled. Pa's gold watch. He remembered being shown it when he was a nipper. Beside it was a guinea – Ma hadn't quite forgotten him after all. He flicked the coin, dropping it in his waistcoat pocket.

'I'd forgot about this. It belonged to my pa; it were his pride and joy. It were promised to me when I was grown. I wonder if it's still working.' He twisted the winder a few times and was gratified to hear a regular ticking.

'Go on then, put it on. You're just the sort who should have a gold watch in his pocket. I can't wait to see you wearing it.'

He pushed the end of the chain through his buttonhole and dropped the watch into the top pocket. He liked the solid feel of it against his chest. He grinned, feeling like a young boy again. 'I reckon I'll be lifting it in and out every five minutes to show it off to folk.'

The waitress appeared with their order and over tea Betty explained what had happened to Sarah. He was horrified to think she had been robbed and beaten, and him not there to protect her. He'd make it his business to find the bastards what done it. He knew their names and where they lived. He might not get Sarah's money back, but they'd get what was coming to them – he'd make sure of that.

'At least we know she's living with Mrs Billings somewhere down St Botolph's Street. It shouldn't be hard to find the house.'

Betty shook her head. 'She won't be there now, Alfie. Remember, she had to be out of the room by Christmas. Don't look so gloomy – we'll find her. Sarah's a survivor.'

'I know what me own sister's like, thank you. We went through enough together over the years. But this ain't the same. It's different for a girl on her own. That parish is little better than the backstreets of London.'

'Shall we go and look right now, Alfie? You pay the bill; I have to go out back a minute. I've still got a couple of hours. It's no more than fifteen minutes from here. That gives us plenty of time to start searching.'

He resented paying out so much for a pot of weak tea and slice of cake his Sarah could have made a lot better. He wasn't sure he wanted Betty along with him; it weren't the sort of place a nice girl like her should go.

Sarah had promised to get in touch with Betty, to send for her belongings, but it were over six months and not a word. Surely, if things had worked out, she would've contacted her best friend? But it was impossible to feel downhearted as he strolled in the sunshine with a pretty girl on his arm. He weren't accustomed to escorting young ladies, but with Betty it were all right – she did all the talking for him. In spite of his worries he found himself laughing at her sallies, enjoying her company more as the afternoon went by.

He enquired at a grocery store and was given the exact direction to the house he sought. They waited together on the doorstep for someone to answer their knock. A large bloke, dressed in the navy woollen of a seaman, filled the doorway. He smiled pleasantly enough.

'Can I help you?'

'It's me sister, Sarah Nightingale – I believe she lodged here last year.'

He looked puzzled. 'I think you've got the wrong house. We don't take in lodgers – there's no spare rooms. Sorry I can't help.'

The door was closing when Betty jumped forward. 'Please, ask Mrs Billings about Sarah. She lived here, last year, when your ma was expecting her last baby. She looked after your little brothers and sister. She was sleeping in your bedroom, I reckon, and left before you got back.'

His expression changed to concern. 'Wait a minute, I'll fetch Ma.'

He left the door ajar and shuffling footsteps, like those of an old woman, approached. He was shocked to see the state of Mrs Billings. She was unkempt, as was the fractious infant cradled in her arms.

'Yes, your Sarah did stay with me. But my husband turned her out when he got back. He locked me and the children upstairs so I couldn't speak to her. I didn't dare go out and look, and then I had a new baby to take care of as well as the other little ones. I've not had time to breathe since then.'

'Look, I'm sorry, mate – I'd no idea about this. If I'd known that bastard had turned a girl out that way, I'd have searched for her, made sure she was all right. I'm Robert Billings. I'll come and help you look.' He placed his arm around his mother. 'You go and sit down, Ma. The boys can take care of Beth. Tell them I'll bring them back a candy twist.'

The woman smiled tiredly and shambled off down the corridor. He came out to join them in the street. 'There's no love lost between me and my father. He's a right bastard, and my younger brother's little better. I only come back to see the kids and give my ma a hand. I hope your sister's came to no harm because of what happened here.'

Alfie liked this bloke. There was no blame on him. 'I'd be glad of your help. I don't know this area; I came from the north.'

Robert eyed Betty's outfit. 'I don't think you should come with us, miss. It's not the sort of place a young lady like you should go.'

Alfie understood exactly the sort of place he was referring to; he'd lived somewhere similar himself. 'I'll take you back, Betty. Robert's right – I don't want you going in them filthy places.'

She stood her ground. 'Don't you dare say I can't go somewhere Sarah might be living. I don't care if my dress gets dirty. All I care about is finding my best friend.' She glared at him and he gave in.

An hour later they'd drawn a blank. People round here were too miserable to take much notice of anyone else's misfortune. No one had heard of Sarah and no one cared either way. He shook hands with Robert and agreed to meet him the next afternoon to resume the search. He walked Betty back, this time taking her to the door.

'Thank you for coming with me, Betty. It makes all the difference knowing Sarah has such a good friend to stand by her.'

'I'd have gone looking on me own, but didn't dare to. I wish we'd found her, Alfie. I have a whole day off at the beginning of June. It's on a Tuesday for a change. Shall I give you her things then?'

'Yes, I've got a decent place. I'll take you round to meet me best friend – Buster. What time shall I be here?'

She tilted her head, working out when she'd be free. 'Be here at half past nine. I'm looking forward to seeing your dog. I like him already. After all he kept you safe in London, didn't he?'

She squeezed his arm, then with a flick of petticoats vanished through the gate. He walked back in a daze, past the castle and into Maidenburgh Street, scarcely noticing where he was. He didn't know if he was worried about Sarah's whereabouts or pleased that he'd met her best friend.

14

COLCHESTER, JULY 1844

Alfie gave a final rub to his table. It weren't too bad in the yard. Most of it was in shade by this time of the day. Betty was in the kitchen baking, but came at his call, a mug of tea in her hand for him. She walked over to admire his work, then sat on the back step, patting the space beside her, inviting him to sit there.

In the last two months she'd taken to dropping in, turning up when-ever she had an hour or two free. She tidied the cottage, baked pies and cakes, ironed his shirts. He was beginning to feel hemmed in; he wasn't ready for this sort of commitment. He liked escorting her around on his arm, walking in the countryside and such, but she seemed to think he was courting her. He weren't ready – not by a long shot.

'I got some tea here, Alfie. What time's Mr Hatch coming to look at the table?'

He couldn't help smiling back. Even with her cheeks flushed from working in the hot kitchen she was still as pretty as a picture. 'Later on this evening, on his way round from collecting rents. If he likes it, I'll get the other work, not have to do so much of the delivering.'

'He'll love it. It's the best bloomin' table I've ever seen. I can't believe how quickly you've got yourself set up here, Alfie. All the sheds mended, a handcart and orders for furniture. Not many men twice your age could have done as well.' She handed him his tea, not suggesting they sit together a second time.

'I ain't sitting next to you, Betty, not until I've had a wash. It's sweaty work, carpentry, and no mistake.' She didn't pull a face, just sat down on her own quite happily. He drained his mug. Funny really, how tea was just as good even when the weather was baking. 'I'll have another one, if there's one going.'

He wished it were Sarah making his tea. He'd still not come to terms with the fact that his sister wasn't going to be found. After two weeks of fruitless searching he'd had to accept she was gone. She must've left Colchester or he would of found her by now. The alternative was unthinkable: that she was dead and lost to him forever.

'I have to go down to The Hythe one of these days to buy me timber; I reckon it'll be cheaper from Hawkins than getting it at that Fred Allcock's near where you work.'

She called from the kitchen. 'It'll make a nice day out. We could take a picnic. I've got a day off at the beginning of next month; I'm not sure which one but I'll tell you next time I come round.'

He wandered up the steps, sniffing appreciatively. 'That smells tasty. What you made me this time, Betty?'

She beamed. 'I've made you steak and kidney pie, and as the oven was already hot, I've made a plum pie as well.' Where she'd got plums from this time of year he didn't like to ask. She'd been bringing stuff round every time she visited; he hoped they were given to her. He'd not want her to lose her position on account of him.

He took his refilled mug, ready to return outside. Was that what her game was? Liquid slopped over his fingers. His eyes narrowed and he stared at her. Had he misjudged her? Was she trying to get herself dismissed knowing he'd be obligated to take her in?

'These things you bring from Grey Friars, you don't pinch them, do you?'

'Don't be daft, Alfie. The housekeeper had a soft spot for Sarah; when she knew I was looking for her, doing a bit of cooking and such for you, she was keen to help. She finds me something left over from the pantry.'

Don't worry yourself – I'm not about to lose my position over any lad. Especially not one as young as you.'

His laugh echoed round the empty yard. He'd been put in his place right and proper. 'Young? I've done more in my almost sixteen years than you have in seventeen. It's a matter of experience, my girl, not how many birthdays you've had.'

She left soon afterwards, promising to come back to let him know exactly when her day off fell. He was glad he'd not been wrong about her. He'd miss her company. Since Robert had returned to sea he'd not had anyone else to talk to. He drew himself a bowl of hot water and took it through to the scullery. He preferred to be clean nowadays, reckoned he washed more than most folk did.

It was hard leaving his supper under the cloth, but he'd not eat until Mr Hatch had been. The flimsy table that had been in the kitchen when he moved in was now in the back bedroom. The one he'd made to replace it was superior in every way. The parlour was furnished. He'd let Betty come with him to purchase the curtains, armchairs and rugs. There seemed little point in leaving the room unused, just waiting for his sister to come and help him choose things.

At least Sarah hadn't been in the workhouse. According to their records she'd never been an inmate. Robert Billings had taken a three-month run on a ship that sailed from Harwich. He didn't like to leave his mother while she was so unwell. Alfie had promised to keep an eye on Mrs Billings. Once he'd got to know her, heard her talking so lovingly about Sarah, he'd really warmed to her.

Next time Robert was home he was coming with him to find the men who had robbed and beaten Sarah. The least he could do was keep an eye on his ma, do a few odd jobs when he was there. She now had a slovenly girl in to help out with the heavy work; better than nothing he supposed. The younger brother was on the same ship as Robert's pa. This meant they rarely met, which suited his friend.

Buster sat up. His low growl filled the yard. The dog hadn't taken to his landlord for some reason. 'Enough of that. You behave yourself.'

Mr Hatch appeared, his smile wary. 'Good evening, Mr Nightingale. Is that the table you've made for me?'

He got straight to business – that's one thing he liked about the man. 'It is, Mr Hatch. There's two side tables and a dresser to look at as well.'

The man ran his fingers over the surface of the table, tipped it to check the joints, then leant his weight on it to see if it would wobble. 'Fine workmanship – plain, sturdy, exactly what I need. Show me the rest. If it's anything as good as this, you've got yourself a deal, young man.'

When he left, they'd shaken hands on an arrangement that should prove beneficial to them both. He was to deliver the table to an address near St Mary's the following day. The only drawback being he'd have to make two side tables, a further kitchen table and a couple of stools, but wouldn't get paid until they were done. He should have asked for a deposit. If he spent out on materials and then didn't sell the items he'd be out of pocket.

He ate his supper, a paper at his side as he scribbled out designs and added measurements. Although he'd not put money in the bank since he'd returned in May, he'd not drawn any out either. He'd made a couple of tables and sold them locally. With this he'd had enough to buy a dilapidated handcart. By the time he'd mended it, and added a little paint, it was as good as new.

That was another problem. Doing carpentry meant he wouldn't have time for delivery jobs. Market days he was run off his feet. He didn't charge much, and although there were others plying their trade, the womenfolk liked his cheeky grin. He reckoned it was Buster that got him so much business; the dog had turned into a right old softy. It was only with Mr Hatch the old Buster showed. That was enough for tonight. He'd turn in early for a change.

* * *

The joint birthday celebrations were well in hand. Dan was no longer distant from his boys. He was eating his lunch with them two or three times a week. His interest made all the difference. There were no more wet sheets or disturbed nights, for which she was thankful. A week before the party he came to find her whilst she was washing up.

'There's something I want to show you in the workshop after the boys are in bed. I'd value your opinion.'

Sarah looked up from the sudsy water. It was the first time he'd followed her into the scullery. 'I've almost finished, then I'll put John to bed. I'm afraid it'll be another hour before Joe and Davie will be asleep.'

He grinned, making him look younger. He'd changed these past weeks, was almost unrecognisable from the man she'd met last year. Sometimes, when he was playing with the boys, rolling around whilst they jumped all over him, he seemed no older than her Alfie. She'd worked out he must be about ten years her senior, but at times like those she seemed the more grown up.

The boys settled. She only had to read two stories before they were ready to sleep. There was usually a cool breeze in the evening coming off the Colne. With the windows open front and back it wasn't too hot upstairs. Mrs Davies had suggested she buy herself a corset, telling her she was letting herself down by not wearing one. Imagine having that on in all this heat! She was still a bit thin – she didn't eat much in summer. Her waist was quite small enough without donning such an instrument of torture.

Dan had knocked up an outdoor table and a couple of benches for the yard. Most days they ate outside now it was so warm. With a nice table-cloth over the top, and a jar of wild flowers the boys had picked along the water meadow, it looked a treat. The children had helped her make a flower bed on the far side, and there was a border full of marigolds, forget-me-nots, daisies and cornflowers to brighten the space. Her spirits lifted every time she came out. One day when she got married, she'd like a real garden, grass to sit on and somewhere to grow vegetables.

She'd also like to have her own things, not be wearing Maria's refurbished clothes. He'd said she could sell them or make them over. It had seemed a pity to sell the clothes when she could make use of them herself. This was why her cupboard was full. Was she becoming the woman whose clothes she was now wearing?

John often called her ma, and although she corrected him gently, he continued. Six months was a long time when you were so small. She headed for the yard, the golden glow of the lamps guiding her to the workshop. What was it that Dan was so eager to show her?

He was standing outside watching the skylarks in his shirtsleeves and bare feet. Good gracious! What had possessed him to work with his boots off? If he dropped a hammer on his foot, it didn't bear thinking of. He turned and smiled.

'There you are, Sarah. Come and see what you think of this.' He threw open the double doors. Her eyes widened. On his workbench was the most wonderful wooden castle; it even had a crenellated top, a draw-bridge, and little windows and doors. Next to it was a box of tin soldiers. She clapped in delight. 'Dan, it's beautiful. I'd no idea you were so skilled. The boys will love it – I can't wait to see their faces.'

'I've been searching out soldiers these past few weeks. Some were a bit battered, but I've touched them up; I don't think they'll know which are old and which new.'

She picked up two and placed them on the platform that ran round the inside. There was also a flight of stairs, and a grand hall with minia-ture furniture. 'I must make wall hangings and curtains. What about adding three flagpoles? I'll make flags to fly on them.' She examined one of the little tin men more closely. 'I shall make them tabards to match their flags, then there will be no arguments when they're playing.'

It was late when they returned to the house. The chickens had gone to roost long ago. She couldn't remember spending such a pleasant evening. 'I've been making them a kite. Mr Davies cut it out for me. They'll be so excited. I can't wait to see their little faces next week.'

That night she fell asleep, her head full of party planning. Mr and Mrs Davies were coming, and Dan had invited a couple of friends from work with their families. That would be nine children and eight adults to cater for. She was making fairy cakes, a blancmange and a junket as well as meat pasties and sandwiches, but pride of place would be the birthday cake.

She'd been horrified how much everything was costing, but Dan had told her to spare no expense. She was going to put sugar paste on the cake and then decorate the top with flowers from the garden. The boys had been making party hats and wanted *blind man's buff* and *pin the tail on the donkey* for the games.

She would soon turn seventeen. Three years ago she'd not been much more than a child – look at her now! Running a household, responsible for three children, and with Nelly to do all the hard work for her.

The boys were beside themselves with excitement about their shared birthday party. They'd put up bunting made from scraps of material. The kitchen table was going out to join the picnic table and all the other chairs. The white sheets were ironed and ready to use as tablecloths and the crockery and cutlery stacked up in the scullery.

A voice called from across the landing. 'Is it morning yet, Sarah?'

'No, John, it's not. It never will be unless you go to sleep right now.'

She brushed her hair in front of the open window. Dan was moving about in the attic. She liked to know he was close by. They'd been lucky with the weather. It hadn't rained for several days; rain would be a disaster because the yard became a quagmire when it was wet.

It wasn't right the master of the house slept up there and she had the best room. Looking around, it was as though Maria had never existed. She'd dropped from their lives like a stone into a pond, the ripples of her life no longer visible. Sometimes Sarah felt she was being dragged down beneath the water herself. The children looked to her for everything. All of them treated her as though she was their mother. Now the fort was completed Dan was spending his evenings in the kitchen with her, no longer sitting on his own in the front room. He'd read her articles from the *Essex Standard* and then they'd discuss the news together whilst she got on with her sewing.

They were settling into a routine. He'd no feelings for her of *that* sort and she most definitely didn't for him. But they were comfortable around each other, shared the same sense of humour. If she was honest she thought he was happier now than he had been when Maria was alive.

* * *

August 1844

Alfie gave Buster a final brush. 'There, you'll do. Want you to look your best today – we're taking you on a jaunt.' Betty would be here soon. The food was ready, and he'd bought the basket specially for today. Hythe was a fair way to walk in this heat, but they'd go along the river path, then the dog could run free until the last half mile.

'Crickey, you made the picnic yourself?' Betty stood grinning in the open doorway.

'Hard-boiled eggs, cheese sandwiches and some of that fruit cake you made. It's a feast. But I ain't carrying the basket – that's your job.'

The walk was pleasant, and they'd picked out a place to stop on their way back for the picnic. 'Will there be anybody to speak to on a Saturday morning, Alfie?'

'I hope so. It's a long way to come for nothing. I need to know if it's worth me while trekking down here; with a full cart it'll be no fun going back up the hill.'

'Go on with you. You're getting fat and lazy like your dog. The exercise would do you good.'

'Ta very much, nice to know I'm appreciated. I'll tell you something – I've not enjoyed a day out so much since I...'

'You went to the opening of the Thames Tunnel. You've told me so often, Alfie, I don't reckon I'll need to go there myself.'

They were like brother and sister. He felt happy with her, treating her as if she was Sarah. He no longer believed she was after him. She had no family nearby and seeing him gave her something to look forward to.

It was after eleven o'clock when they arrived at the bridge. They crossed it and turned down towards Hawkins timber yard. It was quiet, not like a weekday. One of the labourers directed him to a brick building where he would find the foreman. Alfie could see the man he needed was tall with a head of dark curly hair and shoulders even broader than his own; he could see him in the office.

'Betty, I can't take the dog into the yard. Will you be all right waiting here?'

'Go along, Alfie, I'll be fine. No one looks sideways at me with his fine fellow at my feet.' The dog flopped down next to her. Buster had taken a real shine to her, but he weren't sure if it was Betty, or the treats she brought him, that had won him over.

He strode across the yard to bang on the door and was beckoned in. 'I've come to enquire about the price of your timber. I'm a carpenter. Me own yard's in the north, but I reckon it might be worthwhile to bring me cart down here, rather than buy it local.'

The man nodded. 'It will be; the sort of timber you want will come from off-cuts. Dan Cooper, I'm foremen here. Tell me what you're looking for and I'll give you a rough price.'

'Alfie Nightingale, pleased to meet you.'

Cooper's jaw dropped. He looked as if he'd been punched in the guts. 'My God, I can't believe it. Today of all days. Alfie Nightingale, you come with me. There's someone I want you to meet.'

15

COLCHESTER, AUGUST 1844

'Look at this, Sarah, it's nearly long enough to go right across the archway. Can I put it up?' The boy waved at the row of misshapen rags tied haphazardly to a piece of string.

She laughed. 'You're too small, Joe. If I stand on a chair I think I can do it for you.'

The boys hadn't seen their birthday gift yet. The castle would be revealed at the start of the party when all the guests were there to appreciate its magnificence. The boys were wearing the shirts she'd made and very smart they looked too. Today she was wearing a new gown. She'd treated herself to a length of cornflower blue cotton and somehow found the time to get it completed for the birthday party.

'Sarah love, I thought we'd come down a bit early; see if we could give you a hand with anything.'

'You're very welcome, Mrs Davies. Look who's here, boys. They can help you finish off your flags whilst I put the kettle on.'

Dan was working as usual this Saturday morning, but he'd promised to be back before noon, giving himself time to wash and change before the first guests arrived. The party was starting out at twelve thirty – a bit early for a tea party but the boys wouldn't be able to contain themselves until the afternoon. Their excitement might well turn to tears and fractiousness. The kitchen seemed unfamiliar without the central table and chairs now these were outside as well.

Mrs Davies joined her. 'Lovely day you've got for it. Whose birthday is it today?'

'Actually, Joe and Davie have birthdays next week, and John's was last week. Made sense to pick a date in the middle.'

'Is everything ready? Nothing I can do to help?'

'When everyone gets here, I'd be glad to have a hand taking out the food. I can't do it too soon; it's too hot out. The birthday cake's a surprise. I finished decorating it last night after they'd gone to bed. And you wait and see what Dan's made them.'

Mrs Davies glanced over her shoulder to see they weren't overheard. 'Something I need to tell you – it's about you and Dan. There's tongues wagging about the pair of you. Gossip has reached as far as The Prince of Wales.'

Sarah was speechless – why should anyone be talking about them?

'It's like this: you're living here, a member of the family not a servant any more. Folks are saying you're his fancy woman.'

The teapot smashed on the flagstones, sending scalding liquid across her ankle. The boys raced into see what the fuss was about but returned to the yard once sure she was not badly injured. Mrs Davies collected a wet cloth and helped her hobble to the front room, by then it was too late to reply to her outrageous suggestion. She and Dan sharing a bed as well as a house? How could people think such a thing?

Mrs Davies cleared up the mess before sending her husband out to purchase a new teapot; this was one article they couldn't manage without today. There had been the odd sideways look recently, the occasional sly wink or nudge when she'd been out shopping, but she'd taken no notice.

How *could* she have been so stupid? She was even sleeping in the bedroom he had shared with his wife a few months ago. Nelly must have been talking, making something out of nothing. It just hadn't occurred to her to mention that Dan slept in the attic now.

She couldn't think straight, didn't know what to do. She'd promised not to leave unless she was getting wed, but surely he wouldn't want her good name to be destroyed? She couldn't think about this at the moment.

It was the boys' special day – it might well be the last one she shared with them.

Voices outside on the pathway roused her. Dan was here – she'd recognise his laugh anywhere. Then a woman spoke. Surely not? It couldn't be! Betty here? This must be the surprise he'd promised her. Forgetting her worries she rushed through the empty kitchen and into the backyard just as Dan appeared through the archway. Sure enough, walking beside him was Betty, her arm through that of a handsome young man who looked vaguely familiar.

'Betty, I can't believe it – you're the best surprise I could possibly have.' The young man grinned. She rocked back on her heels. It was her Alfie. She'd not known him until he smiled at her.

Ignoring Betty's outstretched arms she flung herself at her brother. He swept her from the ground. He was so tall and handsome. He was supposed to be her younger brother; somehow they'd changed places.

'Sarah, I can't believe it. When Dan said there was someone he wanted me to meet, I'd no idea it was you.' He twirled her around like a small child, her petticoats flying everywhere revealing her bare ankles. It had been too hot to wear stockings this morning.

'Alfie, put me down. Let me give my best friend a kiss.' Then she was in Betty's arms, laughing and kissing, tears of joy streaming down her face. Dan was standing quietly, watching her excitement. 'Dan, I can't believe it. Thank you so much for bringing them. When you said you had a surprise for me, I'd no idea it was something as wonderful as my long-lost brother and best friend.'

'Glad to be of service, Sarah love. I'll leave you to catch up; I'll go in and get myself spruced up. Come along, boys, you can find your ball.'

Fortunately Mr Davies returned, clutching a shiny brown teapot, just in time for his wife to make everyone a cup of tea.

'Come and sit down. Don't use the benches – they're for the children. Use a chair. Where have you been all this time? I can't believe how much you've changed.' She looked across at his smart jacket and saw a gold chain protruding from his buttonhole. 'You've got Pa's watch on. He'd be proud of you – you've obviously done well since you left Colchester.'

Alfie grinned, making him look more like the boy she remembered. 'I'm sorry, I didn't bring anything for the party.'

Betty interrupted him. She seemed to do a lot of that, Sarah noticed. 'We didn't know we'd be seeing you. You don't expect anything, do you, Sarah?'

'Of course not. We can't talk now; the guests will be arriving soon and I've got food to bring out. Everyone should be gone by teatime. Can you stay on till then, Betty?'

Her friend smiled. 'I don't have to be back until nine o'clock. I can't believe my first full day of this year and I find you safe and sound and living with Dan Cooper.'

Sarah's cheeks crimsoned. Betty's smile faded and Alfie's expression turned to a scowl.

'I didn't think to ask what you're doing here. That little one called you ma, didn't he? I can't believe me sister would move in with a bloke without being wed. I'm going to have words with Cooper.'

This was a disaster. 'Please, Alfie, don't. Whatever it looks like, I'm not sharing his bed. He sleeps in the attic; I sleep next to the children. I was housekeeper before his wife died in March. John calls me ma because he can't remember his own any more.'

He sat down, but kept staring at the kitchen door as if he was planning to go in and confront Dan at any moment. Betty reached over and squeezed her hand.

'It's my fault – me and my chatter. I should have thought before I spoke. You're the last person to do anything they shouldn't; in some ways you haven't changed at all.'

The boys erupted from the back door holding their ball. Suddenly, Alfie was on his feet and vanished into the kitchen.

'Betty, this is awful. I only realised today what folks are saying. It didn't occur to me anyone might think I was sharing a bed with my employer. He's not shown the slightest interest in me in *that* way. We're good friends, we get on well together, and that's all there is to it.'

'I believe you, Sarah, but it's not me that matters. You've got two choices: you've either to leave, move in with your Alfie – he's got a lovely little cottage in Maidenburgh Street. He could do with someone to take care of him.'

'Or? Are you suggesting that I must marry Dan if I want to stay here?'

Alfie appeared in the doorway. The day was ruined. Even having her brother and her best friend back couldn't make up for this.

'Dan's in the front room. He wants to speak to you. Go on, it ain't as bad as it looks, I promise you.'

This wasn't the Alfie she remembered. She didn't know him any more. It had always been *her* role to take care of *him*.

Dan was standing by the window, his face in shadow. 'Come in, love, this shouldn't have happened, not this way. But I'm glad it has. I should sit down. I've got to talk to you, and we don't have much time before the guests arrive.'

She folded herself in the armchair, the dark red mark clearly visible across her foot and ankle.

'How did you burn yourself? Let me look.' He was at her side, his hands gentle as he picked up her foot to examine the scald.

'It's not as painful as it looks, Dan. I dropped a teapot and it splashed over me. It's nothing, I promise you.'

He moved across to sit opposite. 'Betty wasn't the surprise I promised you, Sarah. I was going to speak to you this evening, after the party, but things have changed. I shouldn't have left things so long.'

She stared at him, beginning to get his drift. 'You don't have to marry me, Dan. I don't care what other people say. We know there's nothing going on, and anyway, I can move in with Alfie and come here on a daily basis. If I'm not sleeping overnight the gossips will have nothing to talk about.'

'That's the point, Sarah, I don't want you to leave, not now, not ever.' He reached into his shirt pocket and held out a small velvet box. 'Sarah love. Will you marry me? I didn't want to ask you until you were seventeen, but I've no choice now the gossip's started.'

'I'm not sure. I'm not ready to be married to anyone. I don't...' Her voice faded away. She turned away, unable to continue. He was back beside her, taking her hands.

'I understand, love. You don't want me in your bed. *I* don't want any more children. I don't want anything to happen to you. I want to take care of you, keep you safe from harm, but I don't want to share your bed.'

She risked a glance. 'Things can go on as before? The only difference will be I'll have a ring on my finger?' He was marrying her so that she could take care of his children. The boys loved her as if she was their mother. He was giving up his chance of happiness with someone later on, doing it for the sake of the boys and to keep her safe.

He was a good man, a kind and gentle one. It would be madness not to accept. She'd never get a better offer. She didn't love him in *that* way, but he didn't think of her like that either.

'Thank you, Dan, I'd be proud to accept under those conditions.'

He opened the box, removed a pretty silver ring and slid it on her finger. 'There's something else. As soon as we're married, we'll start looking for somewhere else to live. You shall have your own house, with a garden for the boys to play in, where you can grow vegetables and flowers.'

Tears filled her eyes. 'But you have to get to work, Dan. I'll not have you walking miles just so I can live in the country.'

'I thought Greenstead Road would be the place to look. I can walk in from there easy enough. I want you to be happy, want us all to start afresh.'

A dog barked in the yard. 'You must go out, Dan. There's a dog, and the boys will be terrified.'

'That'll be Buster, your Alfie's animal; he's a monster but soft as butter. Listen, they're laughing. I reckon they're playing ball with him. I'm surprised you didn't notice him.'

'I was so shocked to see Alfie and Betty I'd no time for anything else.'

Outside the children were rolling about with the biggest dog she'd ever set eyes on. The animal appeared to be enjoying it as much as they were. Alfie and Betty were chattering to Mr and Mrs Davies and all were clutching mugs of tea.

She looked at Dan, and he slipped his arm around her waist. 'It's for show, love. What we've decided is nobody else's business.' She relaxed against him, and he raised his hand and called for quiet. 'Joe, Davie, John, we've something to tell you, come over here, quickly now.'

The three boys stood in a semicircle gazing at their father. He touched each one in turn. 'Sarah and I are getting married as soon as we can; she's going to be your ma.'

They flung themselves, not at him, but at her. She drew them into her arms. She was doing the right thing; she loved these boys as if they were her own. She'd be comfortable and secure for the rest of her life. Alfie didn't need her – he'd got Betty at his side, hadn't he? Her brother walked across and slapped Dan on the back. Mr and Mrs Davies joined in with their best wishes. Only Betty remained silent; she knew how things were.

The party was a huge success, the cake admired, the castle the best thing anyone had ever seen, the spread more than enough for everyone. By the time the guests departed, each carrying slices of cake, it was getting dark. The boys were exhausted and with Betty's expert assistance they were washed and into their nightshirts within half an hour.

Dan and Alfie cleared away and did the washing-up whilst they were upstairs. Alfie then insisted on taking Dan out to celebrate; after all he was going to be his brother-in-law very soon. Betty was waiting to express her concern, but Sarah was determined to speak first.

'I'm not like you, Betty. I don't have a romantical bone in my body. I never really understood how Jane felt about that groom. I don't think I'm *that* way inclined. Dan's a good man. I shall live in my own house, will be secure and comfortable for the rest of my life. How many other women can say the same?'

Betty shook her head. 'But you don't *love* him. That's all very well at the moment, but what happens if you meet someone and fall for *him* later on?'

Sarah laughed. 'I'll tell you what happens: nothing at all, because if ever I *do* fall in love it will be with my husband.'

'I told you he thought you were a bit of all right when you was robbed and he came to look after you. I reckon it won't be long before you change your mind. I wouldn't say no to a bit of how's your father with him, I can tell you.'

Sarah hastily changed the subject and they spent the remainder of the evening planning the wedding. When Alfie returned with Dan he took her to one side. 'He's a good man, Sarah. He loves you and will make you a fine husband.'

'I'm sure he will or I wouldn't have agreed to marry him. I want to bring the boys up to see your cottage. What about tomorrow? We can come after we have attended church.'

'I've not got enough in to give you dinner – but we'll manage.'

She embraced him and then kissed her friend. They walked off, the huge dog by his side, and she thought they too made a perfect match. Perhaps there would be a second wedding later in the year.

For some reason Dan hadn't come into bid her goodnight but wandered off into the yard again. She made her way upstairs, her heart so full she couldn't remember ever being so happy.

She checked the boys were sleeping soundly and then retired to her own room. Once comfortably settled between the sheets she let her mind wander – thought about what the future might hold. When Alfie had told her that Dan was in love with her she'd thought this was just something that had been said to smooth things over.

Now she recalled all the little things that he'd said and done over the past few months, how happy he'd been, and she began to believe that whatever he'd said, his offer hadn't been one of expedience, but because he truly wanted to spend the rest of his life with her.

A warm glow started at her toes and spread rapidly until she was tingling all over. One day she would share her bed with him, hopefully have a baby of her own to hold in her arms, and be living in the house of her dreams. She was the luckiest girl in Colchester.

Was it possible she already had feelings for him but had been keeping them at bay because of their situation?

There was no rush – she had the rest of her life to fall in love with him.

ABOUT THE AUTHOR

Fenella J. Miller is a bestselling writer of historical sagas. She also has a passion for Regency romantic adventures and has published over fifty to great acclaim.

Sign up to Fenella J. Miller's mailing list for news, competitions and updates on future books.

Visit Fenella's website: www.fenellajmiller.co.uk

Follow Fenella on social media here:

facebook.com/fenella.miller

x.com/fenellawriter

ALSO BY FENELLA J MILLER

Goodwill House Series

The War Girls of Goodwill House

New Recruits at Goodwill House

Duty Calls at Goodwill House

The Land Girls of Goodwill House

A Wartime Reunion at Goodwill House

Wedding Bells at Goodwill House

A Christmas Baby at Goodwill House

The Army Girls Series

Army Girls Reporting For Duty

Army Girls: Heartbreak and Hope

Army Girls: Behind the Guns

The Pilot's Girl Series

The Pilot's Girl

A Wedding for the Pilot's Girl

A Dilemma for the Pilot's Girl

A Second Chance for the Pilot's Girl

The Nightingale Family Series

A Pocketful of Pennies

A Capful of Courage

A Basket Full of Babies

A Home Full of Hope

Standalone

The Land Girl's Secret

Sixpence Stories

Boldwod

Boldwood Books is an award-winning fiction publishing company seeking out the best stories from around the world.

Find out more at www.boldwoodbooks.com

Join our reader community for brilliant books, competitions and offers!

Follow us
@BoldwoodBooks
@TheBoldBookClub

Sign up to our weekly
deals newsletter

https://bit.ly/BoldwoodBNewsletter